Lady Seeker

Children of the Goddess, Volume 5

Prudence MacLeod

Published by Prudence MacLeod, 2024.

LADY SEEKER

First edition. January 13, 2024.

Copyright © 2024 Prudence MacLeod.

ISBN: 978-1927478516

Written by Prudence MacLeod.

Lady Seeker

by

Prudence MacLeod

Finding a Seeker

Lenora Schmidt stood in the driveway staring at the house, dreading going in. This house had been her home for twenty years, but she knew it would be no longer. Not after she delivered the news to her father. She sighed deeply, fighting her desire to run and warring with herself inside.

"He's going to blow his top, you know that," she told herself. "He's going to go bat shit crazy and somebody will pay the price, probably me. I'll be lucky if he doesn't kill me outright. I should run while I can. Hell, I should never have come home at all. No, I owe them this much; Mom, at least. Okay, stay sharp, keep a clear path to the door, and face the music. He's going to blame you for this and you know it."

Her father was a violent man, always had been, given over to fits of temper. He'd managed to stay out of prison because mostly he took out his rage on his wife and children, primarily Lenora. She, on the other hand, had spent much of her young life learning how to duck, lie, hide, and whatever else it took to avoid the beatings. This time she knew there was no way out for her except to run, and that would leave her mother to take the beating. She squared her shoulders and stepped through the door.

"Lenora, you're back," exclaimed her mother. "Wilson, she's back."

"You've been gone for weeks," said a heavyset man in his mid-forties. "Did you find Belinda?" Belinda was Lenora's younger sister, the apple of her father's eye, and she'd been missing for months.

"Yes," Lenora replied softly, staying close to the door. "I found her."

"Well, where is she? Did you bring her home?"

"No, she refused to come."

"Where is she then? I'll go get her myself." He was already getting angry and moving closer to Lenora.

"She's in Los Angeles, but I promised not to tell where."

"What? Just what the hell is going on, young lady? You tell me where your sister is right now." He grabbed Lenora by the front of her jacket, but she squirmed out of it and fell back onto the floor. "Why the hell won't you tell me where she is?" He threw her jacket at her.

Lenora snapped at last. "Because she begged me not to, that's why. You want to know where she is, what she's doing since she ran away from home? She's a porn queen."

"What?" That made him pause.

"You heard me, she's a porn queen. She ran away from home, met up with a guy who was nice to her and he got her into the movies. She actually enjoys her work."

"You're lying, you fucking little bitch. You were always jealous of her. Now tell me the goddamn truth." He punched her hard in the stomach, driving the air from her lungs.

Lenora fought the air back into her body then hurled a movie case like a frisbee. It hit him in the chest. "Look for yourself." She gasped for breath as she struggled to her feet.

"Oh sweet Jesus. Oh dear god." He was staring at the cover on the case and the picture of his baby girl, naked with a penis in her mouth. Lenora made a break for the door, but he grabbed her by the hair and hauled her back. "This is all your goddamned fault," he shouted, as he hit her hard. "You were supposed to look after her, keep her out of trouble. Now look what you've done. You've ruined her."

He kept shouting as he kept punching her. Finally he threw her out into the driveway. "You get the fuck outta my sight, you little whore. Don't you dare ever come back here."

Lenora tried to crawl away. She had a broken arm, three loose teeth, two broken ribs, a fractured cheekbone, broken nose, and both her eyes were closed over. Blood oozed from her broken nose as she tried to crawl away, the sounds of her mother's screams ringing in her ears. She almost made it to her car before her reserves ran out.

She lay there in the driveway, praying one of the neighbors would call the police. In her heart she knew that wouldn't happen. It never did. The whole neighborhood was terrified of her father. She tried to move once more, but her strength was gone in waves of pain.

Suddenly the pain vanished. A vast presence surrounded her, soothing her, and holding the pain at bay. "Who or what are you?" she asked silently. "How are you doing this?"

"*How does not matter, Lenora, my child,*" said a gentle, yet rich and loving, voice. It spoke only in her mind, responding to the questions she thought of, but was unable to utter. "*What matters is, you are badly injured. I can heal you, if you so desire.*"

"Go for it," thought Lenora. "I know you want something, and I'll do it whatever it is. Just get me away from here."

"*I do have a task for you, Lenora, however, that can wait until you're rested and healed. For the moment, I will heal your injuries if you promise to listen fully to my proposal afterwards. Once you can make a decision not based on pain, we will talk. For now, I'll heal you if you promise to listen.*"

"I'll listen to anything as long as I survive. Please get me away from here before he comes out after me."

"*He won't harm you further, I promise. Be still now and I will heal you.*"

Lenora sighed as a wave of sweet loving energy swept through her. She giggled as she felt her ribs and arm shift back into place and knit together. She almost shouted with glee as her energy soared. Her teeth stopped hurting and moved back into place, and then her eyes opened again. She was alone in the driveway. She could still feel the vast loving presence surrounding her, but she was alone.

With a cry of delight, she surged to her feet and sprinted away as the door banged open behind her. She heard her father swearing as he gave chase, but she shouted with glee as she sped on. Lenora felt she could run forever. She fairly flew down the street, across the open field and down to the river. Reaching the bridge, she looked back. Her tormentor had long since given up the race. Lenora danced down the embankment and hid herself from sight. She could still feel the presence with her.

"Okay, I'm like the troll under the bridge now." She sat on a rock beside the sluggish river, breathing deeply. "I think I'm safe enough to talk. Who are you and how can I ever repay you for what you've done?"

"I am Moragah, goddess of Wisdom and Defender of the Weak. From time to time I create a priestess to serve me in special ways. I was looking for just such a person when I found you.

"A priestess? Serve you in special ways?"

There was amusement in Moragah's voice now and it made Lenora smile. She felt so safe and loved in the presence of the goddess. *"It is not quite as you might imagine. I'm familiar with modern religions, but they do not resemble what I need from you in any way. Permit me to show you some of the other priestesses."*

It was like watching a movie, and she was enthralled. Lenora saw a blonde girl fairly flying across the rooftops to drop like a bomb into a street gang. She watched as the girl demolished the aggressors. Next was a dark girl with cold deadly eyes. She stepped out of a wall and destroyed several men who were beating a woman. Next was a small blonde who threw fire from her hands then walked through it to carry a victim away from abusers. The last was an elvish warrior riding on the back of a dragon. When the beast landed she morphed into a woman not much older than Lenora.

"Wow," she breathed. "They're amazing."

"Penny fights brutality wherever she finds it. Kara and Tasha fight to bring justice back to a city that has seen too little of it. And Lady Shadow, Seline, is a hunter. She hunts the bringers of darkness and stops them. She strives to return the balance between the darkness and the light."

"You want to make me like them?"

"Yes and no, Lenora. I have a different task for you, if you are willing to undertake it."

"No dragons, I'm afraid of heights. I'd fall off that monster and break my neck."

Moragah's delight filled her, and she couldn't repress a giggle. *"Very well, no dragons for you. No, Lenora, I've given Seline great power, for her task is the greatest of them all. For you I would give you different abilities. You would be stronger than a dozen men. Your injuries would heal almost instantly. When attacked or under stress you would shift onto combat mode wherein you move at incredible speed and everything else seems to be in slow motion.*

"I need a seeker, Lenora. So many souls and more are lost and abandoned in this world. So many have no resource yet, unknown to them, there are those who love them and search for them constantly. Your task would be to find the lost, both human and other, and reunite them with the ones who love them. For this task you would have the ability to track by scent like a hunting wolf. You would be able to see in the dark, climb easily when it seems impossible to climb, and you would instinctively avoid danger. You would also have a built-in sense of direction. These attributes and more will be yours if you will help me."

"All that and more? And I get to help reunite others with their families? But what if their family is like mine?"

"You would know instantly, Lenora, and would refuse to aid the family. Remember, defend the weak is our main motive."

"Moragah, I feel better right now than I have ever felt before. I'll do it. Oh god, I can't wait to get started."

"There is one more thing."

"Oh?"

"Yes. Once we do this there is no turning back, ever. You will be mine completely. My laws and only my laws will pertain to you. I will possess you and always be with you, experiencing everything you experience. I will

always be with you as a part of you. Also, Whenever possible, I'd enjoy a prayer of greeting at sunrise each day. Is this acceptable to you?"

Lenora didn't hesitate. "Got it. I can do this, and having you as a living part of me would be wonderful beyond anything I've ever experienced."

"Then you are mine, my daughter. Brace yourself for I am told this hurts like hellfire, but it only lasts a moment. And then I will sooth your pain and you will then be Lady Seeker."

Lenora took a deep breath then nodded. Suddenly every cell in her body seemed to burst into flame ripping a blood curdling scream from her lips. The pain was gone before the sound of her scream died on the air. She sat, hand over her heart, breathing deeply.

"It is done, Lady Seeker, my priestess. Be ready, for your abuser approaches even now."

"Oh crap, he'll find me. What am I going to do?"

"What you must, my priestess. I have prepared you. Deal with this man as you see fit."

"I'd like to kill him."

"Then do so with my blessing." So saying, Moragah pulled back and Lenora was alone beneath the bridge, standing on the gravel bar as her father came down the bank and rushed at her.

Suddenly his world went all to hell. She kicked him and broke his leg. She then leaped at him and broke one of his arms. With one hand she gripped his throat and held him up in the air. "Never again, you hear me, never again. If I ever hear of you hitting my mother again, I'll come back and beat you to death. Understand?" She dropped him then walked away, crossing the river on exposed stones, and disappearing up the opposite bank. She didn't even go back for her car.

Getting Started

Lenora had a spring in her step as she strode along the road. An ambulance went screaming by and she hoped it was for her mother, not her father. "Maybe I should go back for the car. No, it's in his name; he'd just report it stolen. All I have is the clothes on my back, but I'm free for the first time in my life."

"*Were you not free before, my child?*"

"No, Lady Moragah, I wasn't. No matter where I went, or what I did, I lived in fear of him. If I came home late, had poor marks, said the wrong thing, ... it never went well. Now I feel free. I don't care what he thinks, or what he does, I'll never go back there, and I'll never have to be afraid of him again."

A drop of rain hit her nose and she stopped to look up. "You're kidding me. Rain? Now?" Several more drops followed the first. "Wait, there's another bridge. Better move it, Lennie." She started to run and was astounded at how fast the bridge appeared. She actually passed an old car.

Safely under the bridge and out of the rain, Lenora called out to her savior again. "Lady Moragah?"

"*I am here, Lenora.*"

"What just happened?"

"*Penny calls it combat mode. When you are threatened or in battle, you speed up and it looks like the world has slowed down. You can also use this method for other needs.*"

"Like getting in out of the rain?"

"Precisely. Don't worry, Lenora, help is on the way. She will be here in a moment."

"Help?"

"Penny, the first priestess I showed you. She's known as Lady Blue. Ah, here she is."

Moragah pulled back and Lenora heard the crunch of tires on the gravel road as the car stopped. A moment later a voice rang out as the rain intensified. "Hey, Lady Seeker, get your butt up here before I drown."

"Coming." Lenora scrambled from her hiding place and swiftly climbed back to the roadside and the waiting car. She found the car running, but couldn't see a driver. She got in.

"Scoot over, you're driving." That voice came from the back seat.

She slid over, strapped on the seat belt, then pulled the old car into gear. "Where to?"

"Any place at all," replied the voice. She could hear someone squirming around in the back. "Okay, watch out, I'm coming up."

An athletic figure slid easily over the seat back and settled into the passenger's seat. "Hi, I'm Penny." She offered her hand and Lenora shook it.

"Wow, you're really Lady Blue."

"I'd say the one and only, but there is another one."

"I heard all kinds of stories when I was looking for my sister."

"Yeah? Scary stuff?"

"Seriously scary stuff, then Lady Moragah showed me more and that truly scared me."

"Aw, come on, I'm not that scary. Lady Seeker, I'm sorry I was late getting here."

"Late?" asked Lenora, as she turned the wipers on high. "I don't understand."

"I was supposed to be here early this morning. It was my plan to stop him before he hurt you, then get you out of there, talk to you about Moragah, then let you make up your mind about what you wanted to do. You weren't supposed to get hurt, and I 'm sorry about that."

"Hey, no worries. Lady Moragah fixed me up and I'm good as new, better even. So what happened to make you late?"

Penny smiled with relief as she saw the twinkle in the girl's eye. "Well, first I ran out of, then stopped for, gas. I broke a nail while I pumped the gas. There was no way in hell I was going anywhere until that was fixed. Then I got a look at my hair in the reflection of the glass and ..."

Lenora was laughing now. "Okay, so now I understand. Don't blame you a bit. Oh, friends call me Lennie. Seriously, now, what's the deal?"

"The deal?"

"What happens now? What am I supposed to do?"

"Now you take a week or so to get used to your new abilities. I'll help you figure out what you can do to maximize those new super powers, then we'll go visit Kara and Tasha, see if their soldiers can help you up the skills more."

"Okay, boot camp for a month, then what?"

"Then I'll drop you off with Shadow and Viper?"

"The dragon rider? No way, forget that. Who or what is Viper?"

"He's a friend of Shadow's. The man is not to be messed with. Anyway, all this is up to you, girl. You're the one in control here."

"Me?"

"Yep, you. That something new for you?"

"Sure is, Penny. It'll be a first."

"Want to talk about it?"

"My father is a brutal man, but you knew that."

"Ah-huh."

"It was always about control. I was always afraid of him, no matter where I was, or what I was doing, or how far away he was, he was still in control. Every decision had the 'what will he do if he finds out?' attached to it."

Penny reached over to gently squeeze the girl's arm. "Never again, girl. Never again. So, what's first?"

"I don't know, I ... oh crap, somebody's lost and hurting." She wheeled the car over and leaped out to hop a fence and race away into the nearby fields. Penny was hard on her heels. Across the field they ran and towards the forest. Just inside the trees they found him, a young beagle pup, his leg caught in a wire snare.

"It's okay, it's okay, I gotcha." Lenora was trying to sooth him and get him free, but the pup was trying to climb into her arms and lick her face off.

Penny snapped off the branch that held him. "Let's go. We can get the wire off him in the car."

Lenora swept the pup into her arms and shifted onto super speed as she raced back to the car. Penny was ahead of her and had the car door open. Once inside out of the rain, Lenora held the pup still while Penny untwisted the wire from his leg. "So, what do we do with him now, Lennie? We can't keep him, not with the kind of life we lead."

"I believe there's a no-kill shelter in the next town. It won't take this guy long to find a new home."

"Maybe he already has one."

"Yeah, he does, but we're not taking him back there. It's not a great place for him."

"And you know this, how?"

"Can't tell you, Penny, but I know it's true."

"Part of the new you," said Penny, smiling at the now playful pup. "How did you know he was there and in trouble?"

"Again, can't tell you. I just felt him and his panic, then I knew exactly where he was."

"Sweet talent, girl. Could be a problem though. We'll have to work on dampening it down."

"What? Why?"

"We keep traveling this road we'll hit a major city in less than two days. There'll be millions of lost, hurt, and panicky, people there. If you want to remain sane you'd better develop some filters and quick."

"Oh crap, good point, Penny. Wait, I'll ask Moragah about this."

"Penny is correct, Lenora, but you do have filters. Just focus on your breathing, focus on your core, and the noise will recede to the background. With a bit of practice you will be able to shut it down and only hear or feel the one you're focused on finding."

"Thank you, Lady Moragah. Penny, she says ..."

"Got it," grinned Penny. "I can hear her too, remember?"

"Right. This is why you're here, isn't it? To help me with stuff like this."

"Yup. We need to work on that before we reach a town or that shelter. Do your thing, girl, find us a campsite."

"Campsite, right. Ah, okay, that way. Here, I'll drive. You entertain Roscoe here."

"Roscoe?"

"It suits him, don't you think?"

Penny chuckled and tickled the pup's belly to make him squirm. "Yeah, it does at that. Right Roscoe?"

Lenora pulled off the main road and, a short way down a dirt road there was a stand of trees beside a stream, an inviting grassy patch just begging for a tent. Penny handed over the pup then set to work at super speed. The tent magically appeared and a nylon fly in the branches protected the fire pit she'd dug. With the fire going, they settled down to dry themselves out. Lenora noticed Penny smiling at her. "What?"

"Lennie, I get the idea you left without packing much."

Lenora sighed and turned her attention to the pup snuggled in her lap. "He was completely out of it, Penny. He would have killed me; there's no doubt about that. I just ran. No packing, no clothes, no money, no car, just what you see here. Dammit, I guess I should have gone back, packed my things, took the car, and cleaned out the bank account. Guess I'm as dumb as he always said."

"Hey now, there'll be none of that. Woman, you'd just had the beating from hell. That man's abused you all your life and naturally you're afraid of him. You were suddenly stronger than ever before, and you ran from that place of terror. I'd have done the same."

"Was it like that for you too?"

"Not quite. Most of the abuse I endured was emotional. When I left home I had a backpack with a change of clothes and thirty bucks."

"Wow, you were lucky." They both laughed and Penny shook a finger at her. "Yeah, that's me, the lucky Penny. Lennie, how far away is that town?"

"About twenty minutes from here, why?"

"You wait here with Roscoe. I'll head into town, pick up some food, a change of clothes for you, and some food for your boyfriend there. Keep that fire going and stay as warm as you can." She rose and got in the car.

Lenora watched her drive away. "Moragah?"

"Yes, my child?"

"Thanks for sending Penny. I'd probably die of pneumonia without her. I should have thought things through more before I just ran away."

"Be at peace, Lenora. You did right. Had you gone back to retrieve your things you'd have to explain how your mother was beaten so badly, your father badly injured, and you without a mark to show for your story."

"Oh crap, I didn't think of that either. I'm such a dummy."

"Those are not your words, Lenora. They are the words of a man who feared he would never be able to control you. You must cease to use those words and phrases to describe yourself. You are actually quite intelligent, and exceptionally resourceful. Did you not track down your sister, even though it took you weeks and carried you across the entire country?"

"Yeah, I guess I did at that. I guess I am resourceful and a pretty smart cookie at that."

"When Penny first went out on her own she took what money she needed from the bullies and abusers she encountered. Later she gained allies who helped her and still do. It will be the same for you. I have no notion who it will be for you, but we will both know when we encounter them. For now, allow Penny to help you."

"That makes sense to do. Moragah, thank you. I guess I should work on my new talents while I'm waiting for Penny to get back."

"Then I will leave you to it." There was a wave of warm, sweet, loving energy and Lenora basked in it. She sighed with contentment as Moragah gently pulled back.

"All right, new abilities. I sensed you, Roscoe, but that was an accident. I need to be able to do it on purpose and I need to be able to focus it. Now, let me see. Momma. Where are you, Momma?" Her body seemed to turn on its own until she was facing a new direction. She called for her mother again and it came more into focus. Finally she could see the woman. She lay in a hospital bed, battered and bruised, casts on her body, and tubes coming out of her. The monitor seemed a bit fuzzy, but by concentrating Lenora was able to see it. Her mother's heartbeat was strong.

She then shifted her awareness to her father. She fought down the anger and fear and concentrated. He was in the hospital too, casts on the bones she had broken, and his good arm shackled to the bed. A policeman was standing guard. Lenora sighed with relief then shifted her attention to her sister. A moment later she blushed and shook off the image. Her sister was obviously enjoying her work. All was well there.

"Okay, so now who? Oh, Penny." Even as she spoke the name aloud she turned toward the road and got a clear visual image of Penny. She was in a grocery store, buying supplies. Lenora smiled and released the image. She gently scratched behind a floppy ear and thought. "Now who? I need to practice."

She did practice, checking in on several of her former school mates. After that she squared her shoulders and called up the image of the dragon rider. That pulled her in another direction. She saw a woman with red hair sitting in a big chair, reading a book. A small dragon was at her feet and a fairy was looking over her shoulder.

To Lenora's great surprise the woman suddenly looked up, her eyes searching until it seemed like she had made eye contact. She tilted her head for a moment then gave Lenora a bright smile. Startled and frightened, Lenora broke contact. "Moragah, she could see me."

"Yes, Seline saw you. She asked me who you are. I told her you were practicing. She said to come to her, and you'll get all the practice you need."

"Should I? Should I go there?"

"You could do that, if you wish."

"I get the impression you have something else in mind for me. That's why you sent Penny to help me instead of her. Am I right?"

"Yes, your insight serves you well, Lenora. However, I won't influence you. You decide what you want to do."

"Moragah, you told me you wanted to create a seeker. You have something or someone special you want me to find, don't you?"

"There is something. I suppose I should say, someone, at this point. However, Lenora, first you must hone your abilities. Once you're ready we'll discuss this again. Be assured, my priestess, I will not force you to do anything you prefer to avoid. When the time comes you will have free will to decide your own fate."

"Now you're scaring me." The vast presence of Moragah enveloped her again, filling her with feelings of being loved and cherished. "Oh god, I love it when you do this."

"Be at peace, Lenora. Stay focused on the moment before you. The future is ever in flux and every decision you make changes things. Deal with whatever is before you and let the rest unfold as it should."

"Okay," sighed Lenora. "That makes sense to do. Ah, here comes Penny now."

Penny hopped out of the car and brought the bags to Lenora. "Hey, the fire's nearly out."

"Yeah, I ran out of wood."

"What about that stick?"

"That's a dog toy. If I reach for it he thinks I want to play tug o' war. I was afraid to put it in the fire. He might burn himself trying to get it back."

"You can't have all the firewood, you little monster." Penny flipped him over and started rubbing his belly. "Lennie, you change into dry clothes, and I'll get more wood from the trunk of the car. I picked up a couple of bundles at the gas station."

Lenora thanked her and slipped inside the tent to change. The sports bra and panties were a reasonable fit and the new sweats were warm and fuzzy. There was a new jacket as well. She came back out to find Penny feeding a raw hot dog to Roscoe. "Penny, I can't thank you enough for the clothes."

"All my pleasure. So, want your hot dogs raw like this guy or should we cook ours?"

"I think cooking might be the way to go."

Penny grinned and passed her a long fork and a package of hot dogs. "So, you were practicing while I was gone."

"Yeah. I saw you buying groceries. I checked in on my family, too. Did you know when I saw you?"

"I thought I felt eyes on me, but couldn't be sure. Why?"

"The dragon rider saw me. She looked right into my eyes. Scared the heck out of me."

"Seline's a bubble of fun, Lennie, but she's almost a goddess in her own right. Scares the hell out of me when she shifts into Shadow. Moragah sent her against some pretty heavy stuff, but she equipped her for the task. You and I have super powers compared to normal people. Seline has super powers compared to us. Relax, girl. You'll like her."

"Oh yeah? You've actually met her? Did she take you for a ride on her dragon?"

"Nope, but she let me hide out for a few days and shared her library. Oh man, that library is so awesome. Lennie, don't be afraid of Seline. She's a sister; she's one of us."

"Sisters. I guess I do have big sisters now. All my life I was the big sister, always looking out for my younger sister. I'm not used to the idea of somebody stronger than me actually looking out for me."

"Well, you'd better get used to it. We're here, all of us, and although none of us started out to be this, we're all warriors. All except you."

"All except me?"

"Oh you'll have your battles, and you're well equipped to fight them, but I get the feeling Moragah has a different job in mind for you."

"What do you mean?"

"Lennie, any one of us could track most people if we wanted to. Seline especially. So, why create a seeker?"

"I have no idea."

"As I said, any one of us could track just about anybody if we wanted to, but it would take time. Your skills cut that time down to almost nothing. I think, once you're ready, Moragah will want you to work with us, speeding things up."

"What do you mean?"

"Well, first there was me, then came Kara. Mai was the third. She got into trouble. Both Kara and I dropped everything to try to get to her in time, but we were too late. Mai was already dead before I found her, and because of that hunt, Kara was almost too late to save Tasha. Lady Justice. If you'd been with either of us we could have known exactly where to find Mai and maybe we would have got there in time."

"That makes sense."

"I'm just speculating here. There's no way to know the mind of our goddess, but She will have a strong reason for creating a seeker."

"Okay, so I need to sharpen up all my skills as quickly as possible, right?"

"Right. We start first thing tomorrow. Right now I want another hot dog before Roscoe gets them all."

They ate in silence for a few moments. Warmed by the fire and the food, the dog settled down between them and went to sleep. Lenora gently stroked his fur. "Wish I could keep him."

"That wouldn't be fair to him, Lennie. Not with the life we lead."

"Are you so sure? I've seen lots of homeless folks with dogs."

"How many of them are chasing bad guys, getting shot at, or being hunted by the police? The dog would be a dead giveaway to the hunters, plus he'd try to defend you and ..."

"Okay, okay, I get it. I can't keep him."

"Lennie, I'm sorry."

"No, you're right, Penny. You're right. It's one of those things, you know? I always wanted a dog, but wasn't allowed to have one."

"It's not a matter of allow my sister in Moragah. It's your decision to make."

"But he'll be a lot happier and safer with a stable family?"

"Ah-huh. Our lives can be quite unstable at times."

"Penny?"

"Mmm?"

"Thanks."

Penny smiled and passed her another hotdog. "So, you can find your family and friends. You can locate the sisters in Moragah. Now we need to move on to more difficult targets."

"What do you mean?"

"Someone you've never seen or heard of before."

"Right, because that'll be what I'm doing all the time, looking for people and things I don't know anything about. Okay, give me something."

Penny grinned. "She's in her seventies, five foot eight, a hundred thirty pounds, some natural blonde still in the silver hair, mischievous blue eyes."

"Who is she?" asked Lenora, smiling.

"My grandmother."

"Name?"

"All right, but you must never speak that name aloud."

"Protecting the secret identity?"

"Yes, that and protecting her. Her name is Magda Larson."

Lenora closed her eyes and tried to picture the woman in her mind. "Magda Larson, where are you, sweet lady?" she whispered. It took a moment, but she felt a slight pull. She turned in that direction and it became stronger. She raised her arm and pointed, moving the arm from side to side until she felt the strongest pull. "That way. She's far away in that direction. I can't see her, but I feel that she is fine and thinking about you. New York, she's somewhere in New York.

"That's as close as I can get from here. If we go to New York I bet I could find her from there."

"Damn, you're good, girl," laughed Penny. "Yes, she lives in New York. Okay, here's another. Woman, gorgeous, thirty-two, light brown hair, blue eyes, athletic, strong willed, and a deadly kisser. Her name's Tara."

It took a moment, but Lenora smiled. "New York, but a long way from the first lady. She's lonely for you. She your partner?"

"Yup. Okay, now for the tougher stuff. Woman, about five-five, maybe one hundred thirty in weight, brown hair, eyes ..."

"Whoa, that had power in it, Penny. Who is she?"

"My birth mother. I was adopted by the Larson ladies as an adult."

"Okay, gotcha." Lenora focused, reaching out with her mind, her new senses. Finally she felt a pull and turned to point. "That way, closer, in a bar, not doing so good. Penny?"

"That fits, keep going."

"Okay, pulling back a bit, small city, mid-west, Paxon. She's in Paxon."

"Bingo, Lennie. You up for the toughest of all?"

"Sure. Penny, what's going on?"

"We're testing your new abilities."

"We're doing more than that, aren't we?"

"Yeah, I guess we are. Sorry. Didn't mean to make my shit your problem."

"Talk to me, Penny."

Penny sighed deeply then threw another stick on the fire. "When I was born my father named me Penny because my birth cost him his last cent, so he always said. He left us on my fifth birthday, and I haven't seen him since. I just suddenly wondered if ..."

"Describe him as best you can."

"Lennie, you don't have to ..."

Lenora patted Penny's arm. "Describe him."

"About six foot, skinny as I remember. His name is Jack Preston. Oh, he has a small scar on his right cheek."

Lenora focused. Minutes passed and Penny didn't disturb her. Perhaps it would be better if she failed. She didn't though. She turned towards the north west. "Seattle," she said softly.

"What aren't you telling me, Lennie?"

"I saw a graveyard, Penny, and a small stone. He died in '99."

Penny nodded slowly, pressing her lips tight together for a moment, but not a tear was shed. "Thanks, Lennie. At least I have some closure on that one."

Lenora gently squeezed Penny's arm. "I'm so sorry, Penny."

Penny patted the hand on her arm. "Don't be. Now I can stop wondering, imagining possible reunions, etc. I can let that one rest now. You did me a big favor, girl. Lennie, this will most likely be a big piece of your job in the future."

"I need to toughen up?"

"No, you need to keep your compassion, but you'll need to keep a bit of distance, too."

"A balancing act?"

"Lady Shadow would tell you it's all about balance. You need to keep a foot in both worlds. Get some sleep. I'll take first watch."

"First watch? Right. I have to learn how to live on the run. Wake me so I can take a turn?"

"Count on it," replied Penny. She didn't though, she let Lenora sleep through the night.

Pushing the Bubble

Morning came and Lenora awakened. Seeing it was daylight she hurried into her clothes and rushed outside to find Penny cooking breakfast. "Hey, you were supposed to wake me for a turn at watch."

Penny grinned and stirred the fire. "No worries. Roscoe took your turn."

"No fair, Penny. I should share the hard stuff too."

"Okay, so you can clean up from breakfast then take down the tent."

"I'll do that, but you have to get some sleep while I do."

"That's a deal I can live with. Looks like the sun's coming out. Want to greet the Lady before we eat?"

"Sure. Can you teach me how?" She did. Penny smiled as she taught Lenora the morning prayer as she had taught it to the bloodline. Moragah favored them with a wave of loving energy then Penny crawled into the back seat of the car and went to sleep.

While Penny slept Lenora cleaned the camping equipment then took down the tent. There was a stream nearby and she took her clothes from the day before to wash them, but try as she might, the bloodstains wouldn't come out. Eventually she gave up, played a game of chase with Roscoe then settled down under a tree to practice. She was still at it when Penny awakened.

Penny trotted off into the trees to relieve herself then returned smiling. "Wow, you're tidy," she said as she saw the camping gear piled neatly beside the car. "I'm taking you camping again for sure. Hey, what's wrong?"

"It's my clothes, Penny. I can't get the blood stains out of them. What am I going to do?"

"Go shopping, of course. We need to push you a bit today anyway, might as well do some shopping while we're at it."

"I can't. I haven't any money."

"I do, lots of it," said Penny as she stowed the camping gear in the car. "Come on, my treat."

"Well, okay, if you're sure."

"I'm sure. Let's go." She tossed Roscoe into the back seat then got in behind the wheel. Lenora got in the other side. "Okay, here's the deal. First you find a shopping area where you can find clothes, everyday stuff, comfortable yet easy to run and jump in."

"Okay, that way. Back to town. The mall is on the other side."

"All right, should we drop Roscoe at the shelter first?"

"Okay, if I have to." Lenora sighed and stroked the pup's head.

Penny patted her hand. "I'm sorry, Lennie, but you know we have to. Now, I'll drive slow. I want you to focus on turning it down. There will be need and desire everywhere and you can't help them all. Focus on tuning it out. Let me know if it is getting to be too much and I'll turn around and back off for a while."

"Okay, got it. Penny, should we go back to my house so I can get my backpack and some clothes? The place will be empty now."

"Cops might be watching it. I'll take you shopping, don't worry."

"I don't want to be a burden and ..."

"Lennie, between you and me, I have plenty of resources. Come on girl, let big sis help you out."

"Well, okay, if you're sure."

"I'm sure. Focus now, we're getting close to town."

Lenora was well aware of that. It was battering at her senses already. Silently she called out. "Moragah?"

"I am here, Lenora, my daughter. You are troubled."

"There are so many, and I can't process it. Please tell me how to control this."

"Perhaps Roscoe could help you."

Lenora felt the amusement in Moragah's voice then the goddess pulled back again. With a soft whimper the pup wriggled into her lap. Instantly her attention went to him, and the noise of the world's needs vanished.

"I guess I don't have to ask directions to the shelter, do I?"

"I need him, big sister. In time I'm sure I'll be able to do this on my own, but for now, I need him."

"Right. Skipping the shelter and heading for the pet shop. We need stuff for him too."

"This will really cramp your style, won't it?"

"I'll adapt. We're not trying to save the world here; we're helping you learn to use your new abilities. Roscoe, you've just been promoted to assistant tracker." The dog wagged his tail happily and Penny smiled at him.

They reached the town and Penny drove slowly as they approached the shopping mall. They didn't get there. A woman approached the car as they waited at a red light. She tapped on the window and when Penny rolled it down she passed in a leaflet. "Please, take a look at this picture. Have you seen this girl? She's been missing for days. Please help me find my daughter."

Lenora's senses went off like skyrockets. The dog licked her face and shocked her out of it. "Get in the car."

"What???"

"Get in the car, woman. We'll help you, but we can't talk here." The woman got in the back as someone behind them leaned on the horn and began to swear.

Penny drove through the light and parked in the first spot she could find. "Lennie?"

"I'm good, Penny. I can do this. I need to do this. We learn by doing, right?"

"All right, you're up."

Lenora turned to the woman. "Tell me what happened."

"It's been two weeks and the police haven't found her. I don't think they tried very hard. Connie ran away with her boyfriend. She's only sixteen. Please, if you know where she is ..."

"Give me a minute." Lenora gazed at the picture on the leaflet. She began to muse aloud. "Talk to me, Connie. Where are you? Come on girl, where are you?" Suddenly she flung out her arm and pointed south. "That way. I need a map."

"We've got GPS ..."

"Useless without a destination, I need a map of the state. She's still in this state. She's alive, but not happy. I need a map, that or we just head out in that direction until I can pinpoint her location."

"Right, gas station, they might have one." Penny pulled out into traffic again then drove to the gas bar. Lenora filled the tank while Penny went inside to pay and buy a map.

She came back and they spread the map out on the hood of the car. Lenora stabbed the map with her finger. "There, she's there somewhere."

"Okay, the closest road is here," mused Penny. "Let's go."

"Who are you people?" The woman in the back seat had Roscoe in her lap now. "Are you a psychic or something?"

"Yeah, I'm really good at finding stuff, people, dogs, you know. Next right, Penny." Penny made the turn. "Tell me more about Connie."

Penny drove on for about an hour then Lenora pointed to a dirt road. They found a cabin and a car. The car had been burned out and the cabin was empty, but Connie's sweater was there. "That way," said Lenora, pointing into the forest. She took the sweater then inhaled deeply.

"What are you doing?"

"I can follow a scent as well as any dog." Lenora stooped and gave the sweater to Roscoe to smell too. "Come on, partner, let's get to work." The scent was faint, but she could follow it. It must have been stronger down near the ground because Roscoe got the idea then set off with a will.

"Stay here," said Penny, as she started after them.

"I'm coming with you."

"Keep up then." Penny sprinted after them. Roscoe was running now, and Lenora was easily pacing with him. Cursing under her breath, Penny slowed down so the woman could keep her in sight. Eventually they lost the trail.

"Where did they go?"

Penny let her frustration show. "I have no idea at all. I told you to stay behind so I could keep up. Relax, woman, I'm not angry, just frustrated." At that point they heard the dog bark as he charged out of the trees. "Hey, Roscoe, where's Lady Seeker? Find Seeker, Roscoe." Wagging his tail happily, he turned and raced back into the trees on a different trail. They followed and soon found Lenora climbing up out of a ravine.

"She was in bad shape," she said as she reached the top and stood up. "Moragah healed her and she's sleeping now. There's no sign of the boyfriend. Do you think we should look for him?"

"Up to you, Sis."

"Well, I'll need Connie awake for that. Have you got any water with you? She's been down there quite a while. She'll need water."

"Right here in my pocket." Penny stepped off the cliff and dropped the twenty feet to the ground below, landing in an easy roll.

"Show off." Lenora grumbled, as she turned and swiftly climbed back down to Penny's side. The girl was awake and drinking greedily from the water bottle. "How are you feeling, Connie?"

"Good." She shyly passed the empty bottle back to Penny.

"All right," said Lenora. "It's time to get you up out of here. Climb on my back and I'll give you a piggyback ride to the top."

"Piggyback? You're going to climb that with me on your back? How the hell do you plan to do that?"

"Easy money, I'm a rock climber. Come on, hop aboard the elevator and up we go."

"Okay, but you're going to get us both killed." The girl put her arms around Lenora's neck from behind.

"Lock your legs around my waist, I'll need my hands for climbing."

Penny swarmed up the face of the cliff and was there to help them at the top. Lenora climbed easily, amazed at her own sense of strength and ability to find hand holds. Moragah had said she'd be able to climb sheer walls and now she fully believed. This was almost too easy. At the top Penny lifted Connie off her and dropped her in her mother's arms.

"Mom, oh god, Mom, I'm so sorry."

"Hush now, Connie, it's all right. I've got you back and everything's all right."

"Donnie, he's dead, Mom, they killed him and..." The girl began to sob uncontrollably.

"There's no time for this," said Penny. "We have to get out of here. You need to get her home and we need to get far away from here."

"What? Why? There's a reward and Connie's father will want to thank you. I ..."

Penny shook her head. "No. Ma'am, we're wanted by the police. We dare not be anywhere near the two of you. Connie, tell me what happened?"

The girl sniffled as she tried to get control of her emotions back. "We were in the cabin. I thought it would be so perfect, so beautiful, but all we did was fight. One day two men came. They'd been drinking and decided they wanted me. Donnie told me to run then he tried to fight them. One had a knife. I ran away, but I heard him screaming. Oh god, Donnie."

Lenora had turned away, her eyes slightly out of focus. "He's not there."

"What?"

"He's not there, in the cabin." She turned and faced a new direction. "He's there, back in town, in the hospital. Alive, but barely."

Penny started back toward the cabin. "Let's go." When they reached the car she turned to the mother. "Got a phone with you?"

"Yes."

"Call someone to come for you. Tell whatever story you need to. Hell, tell them the truth. However, when you speak of us..."

"I never saw you before and don't know who you are."

"There's more." Penny began drawing blue spirals on her face and arms. "We were both wearing these spirals. I'm Lady Blue and this is Lady Seeker. We both had the spirals. You can't identify us, help with a drawing, or anything at all like that."

"Lady Blue," breathed Connie. "Oh my god. I've heard all sorts of things about you."

"Some of it might even be true. So, we're good here? You'll be alright until someone comes for you?"

"Yes, of course," replied the girl's mother.

"Then we're gone. Get in the car, Roscoe." Wagging his tail, the dog happily jumped in and climbed onto Lenora's lap." The woman was already on the phone as the car sped away.

Penny drove in silence for a while. Finally Lenora broke the silence. "So, Big Sis, how did I do?"

"Do? Woman, you're amazing. Totally amazing. You rocked it, girl. Sorry about your shopping trip. That'll have to wait for another town."

"Yeah, I kinda figured that. It's okay, we did a good thing and that makes it right."

"Yes, it does. So, how did it feel?"

"It felt good to help them."

"Not what I meant, girl. How did it feel when she first spoke to us. You looked like you'd been hit by a truck."

"It was almost like that, Penny. It was like skyrockets went off in my head. Up until then I had a handle on it. There was need everywhere, and desire. I could live there a year and not even get close to helping everybody. People had lost their keys, pets, clothes, phones, and so on forever. By focusing on Roscoe it all became like white noise, but she really lit me up and I knew. We had to help her."

Penny nodded slowly. "There're some wet wipes in the glove box. Want to hand me one so I can get the grease paint off my face?"

"Huh? Oh sure."

Lenora passed over the wipe and Penny cleaned herself as she drove. "So, you have a signal now. You know the mundane stuff and you know the stuff you really need to pay attention to. We need to sharpen that. However, I promised you a shopping trip and I'm hungry. You've got the map, where's the next town?"

They found a roadside cafe near the interstate and stopped for a meal. Roscoe put up a fuss when they left him in the car. Lenora went back to calm him, and Penny went inside to order the food. It was already on the table when she arrived. "How's our boy?"

"He's not happy, but he's settled down a bit. Penny, can we stop at a campground for the night?"

"Sure, why?"

"Well, if we make him sleep in the car he'll be more likely to accept it as his den so I can actually leave him for a short time."

"Okay, makes sense. There's something else we have to do tonight, and a campsite is just the place to do it."

"Oh?"

"We have to burn those blood-stained clothes."

"Why?"

"Right now you're just a girl who ran away from a brutal man. If the police find those clothes with blood all over them ..."

"They might think I'm the one who attacked them both. Crap. God I'm glad you're here to help me." Penny just smiled and patted her hand.

They took the highway to the next town then went shopping. Lenora now had a handle on the impressions assaulting her mind. She kept an image of Roscoe beside her even when he had to remain in the car. When they stopped for the night Lenora had two fresh outfits in her new backpack and the hundred dollars Penny had given her for emergency money. Roscoe had a new collar.

The next day they found a bigger town and took a motel room. They spent the day wandering aimlessly around the streets. "Penny, what are we doing?"

"Conditioning your senses. How are you doing?"

"Good. I'm good. There's a lot of noise, but I can push it back and ignore it."

"Anything lighting you up?"

"A couple of those missing children posters on the power poles gave me a small hit, but nothing like Connie's mom did."

"Okay, we'll push on to a bigger city tomorrow. Once you're comfortable with that we'll go home to meet the family."

"The family?"

"Mamma and Grandmamma. We'll spend a few days in New York to toughen you up a bit then we'll start looking for ways to sharpen your skills."

"Oh, how do you plan to do that?"

"You'll see."

"Oh yeah, it's like that, is it, sister?"

"Yup."

"You're going to be mean to me, aren't you?"

"Nope, but I will teach you how to run free. There's lots of names for what I do, but I know it as free running. I'll teach you. It'll get your body into shape like never before, and it'll sharpen your mind."

"Cool. I think I'd like that."

THEY'D SETTLED INTO a campsite the next night and made a spare meal. Roscoe was snuffling about and Lenora was gazing into the fire where the last remnants of her blood-stained clothes were slowly dissolving in the flames. She sighed and stirred the coals.

"That was a deep sigh, girl. You okay?"

Lenora nodded. "Yeah, I'm good. I was just thinking, that's the last vestige of my former life that I have. I guess I'm all brand new now. A fresh start. A clean slate sort of thing."

"Yeah, well, I'd say you're off to a great start. That was the other day. Usually, even when I'm helping or saving someone, somebody else has to pay the price, you know? Making a save without hurting anybody else is a rare thing for me. I liked it, it felt good."

"Yeah, it did, didn't it?"

Penny smiled at her. "Get some rest, Seeker. We'll be in New York tomorrow and you'll get to meet the family."

All in all, Lenora stayed with Penny in New York for three months. In all that time she rarely rested. They started every day with free running, and then hand-to-hand combat practice with Tara Montrose instructing. After that, they practiced finding things, things and people. Lenora would find them and then Tara would call the police and make an anonymous tip. Lenora was getting sharper at her hunting, and she always took Roscoe with her.

Lenora also fought her first few battles as she helped Lady Blue stop muggings, break up street brawls, and a few cases of domestic violence. The training with Penny had taken the soft edges off her and made her stronger.

It was to be her last hunt with Penny before she went out on her own. As usual, Mary Larson drove them down into the city then let them out. She took a deep breath to clear her mind. "Okay, what's the target?"

"We walk down the street. First poster you see is your target."

"Got it. Let's get to work." It was late that night before they returned home. There were several dead bodies back in the city and a young prostitute was on a bus home, a trip she had feared she would never be able to make.

The Adventure Begins

Early the following morning Lenora said her goodbyes to the Larson Ladies, as she called them. Penny was fussing over her like a mother hen.

"Okay, got your new ID?"

"Yep."

"Credit cards?"

"Yep."

"Got enough money?"

"Yes, Mom," replied Lenora.

"Okay, here's your keys."

"My keys? Penny, I can't take your car."

"Not my car, sis. I got it for you when Moragah first called me to help you. Besides, you can't take Roscoe on the bus."

"Yeah, I guess you're right about that. Gods, Penny, I'm going to miss you."

Penny laughed then hugged her fondly. "I'll miss you too, Little Sis. Take care and stay in touch."

"I will, I promise." She climbed aboard the car and settled into the driver's seat. Penny stood and waved goodbye until the car was out of sight. Lenora was now officially on her own.

Two days later, Lenora and Roscoe sat beside a small campfire having a conversation about the future. "I know, Roscoe, but you ate it all. No, we have to ration ourselves a bit. Okay, but this is the last one." She fed him another hot dog. "You know, I'm willing to admit, I enjoyed my time living in New York with the Larson Ladies. Penny doesn't seem to mind sleeping in a tent or the back seat of a car, but I prefer sleeping in a bed, and I know you do, too. So, it comes down to this. We're running low on money."

The beagle laid his chin on her lap and gazed adoringly up at her with those huge puppy eyes. Lenora smiled and stroked his head, rubbing gently just behind the ears. "As I was saying, we need a job, Roscoe. A job will provide a bed and breakfast for both of us every day, and I want that. I know Moragah has something special in mind for me, but she's not talking. I assume by that, I'm not ready yet.

"Now, the plan is to not starve while we're waiting to be ready. We could go mooch off Lady Justice for a while, but that's going from the campsite to the sewer. Not a big step up in my book." The dog groaned and rolled onto his back, presenting his belly for rubbing. Smiling warmly, Lenora obliged.

"We could go hang out with the Dragon Rider, but she's a bit scary, and I wouldn't want you to get eaten by a dragon. So, it looks like we're on our own here." She tossed the last piece of firewood on the coals.

"Okay, a job. So, what are our assets? Well, you're cute as can be, a great snuffler, tail wagger, a king at tug-o-war, and unequaled at mooching. Not a lot of job opportunities there. Now for me. I have a high school education and a bit of experience at flipping burgers." The dog wriggled against her leg again to get her attention. She resumed rubbing the offered belly.

"Yeah, I'm sure my sister could get me a job with her in California. Not my thing. So, where does that leave us? Well, my furry friend, that leaves us with the goddess given super powers. So, how can they help us get a job? I find stuff, just like you do, Sir Beagle. I can follow a scent, see in the dark, climb walls, locate people psychically, and I'm really strong and fast. What does that sound like to you? As a job description, I mean.

"What's that you say? What? We should be bounty hunters? Now why didn't I think of that? Yes, my fuzzy boy, that's the perfect job for us. Tomorrow we'll go see if we can scare up any work as bounty hunters before we run out of dog food money. Come on, one last game of tug-o-war before we go to bed. Go fetch the toy."

The dog sprang to his feet and hopped into the back seat of the car, reappearing with the tug toy. There followed a contest of strength and wills that carried them around the campsite for quite some time. Finally the dog won and settled down by the fire to chew contentedly on his prize. Smiling with delight, Lenora sat beside him and stroked his back.

"Lady Moragah?"

"I am here, my priestess."

"Is that okay to do? Try to find work as a bounty hunter?"

"Considering your particular skill set, I think it would be the perfect solution. By doing so, you sharpen and hone your skills as well as meet your own needs. It also leaves you independent to go where you please or where needed."

"Thank you, Lady Moragah. I guess I should get some sleep if I want to look awake enough to do the job tomorrow."

"Then be at peace, my daughter. I will guard your rest this night."

Next morning Lenora stood facing the rising sun, arms held high, and said her morning greeting to her goddess. After that Roscoe got his breakfast. All she had was a bit of beef jerky. Lenora would save all her money for gas.

She drove to the nearest city, about a half a tank of gas away. She topped up the tank, took Roscoe for a short walk to do his business then ran a comb through her hair and walked into the police station. There was a bored policeman behind the desk. "Can I help you, Miss?" He rubbed his hand over his balding head. "Damn it's hot today."

"Yeah, sure is. Is there a bulletin board with wanted posters on it?"

"Right over there." He pointed in the general direction of the far wall. "You looking for somebody in particular?"

"Anybody with a reward on his head."

"Reward? You a bounty hunter? Girl, you must be a lot tougher than you look."

"You have no idea." She grinned as she studied the posters. Lenora saw plenty of offers of rewards for information leading to an arrest. Far too slow. She needed cash now. "Got anything that pays up on delivery?"

"Girl, what you're looking for is a bail bondsman. They pay cash on delivery for the return of bail jumpers. I should warn you; more than one bounty hunter has been killed on the job, and then there's the other."

"Other?"

"If you're a bit too exuberant when you make a capture you can get sued by the perp. They usually win those cases."

"You're joking."

"I'm not. Oh, hey, you're in luck. Here comes Morty. Hey, Morty, this gal's a bounty hunter. She's looking for work."

The well dressed man turned to her and gave her a professional smile. "Morton T. Gluagar at your service."

"They call me Lady Seeker," she replied as she shook the offered hand. "I can find anybody, any time, anywhere. Got anything for me?"

"I do, but you'd better have partners, big tough partners."

"Tell me about him. I assume it's a man I'm looking for."

"Yes. His name is Billy Franks. He's a big boy and extremely violent. Beat his wife to death in a domestic dispute then jumped bail on me. You and your people bring him in it's worth ten thousand."

"Cash?"

"If you want."

"I do want. Okay, let me see a minute." Lenora closed her eyes and began whispering the man's name. "Come on, come on, where are you, Billy Franks. Talk to me now, where are you, Billy Franks?" She turned away from the two men and faced south.

The man called Morty gave her a strange look. "What are you doing?"

"Finding your guy. I'm a psychic. Hush now, let me work. Where are you, Billy? Okay, so there you are. Does he have a scar over his right eye? Big fella? Red hair?"

"Sounds like him," grinned the policeman.

"Okay, Mister Gluagar. You go to the bank and get the cash. I should be back before sundown." With that, she walked out of the police station.

The two men watched her go in silence. "What the hell just happened?"

The policeman grinned at him. "You just hired a psychic bounty hunter, Morty. Between you and me, I'd go to the bank and get her cash. I'm betting there's a couple of big bad boys waiting outside of town."

"I sure hope so, for her sake. Billy Franks is the meanest bastard I ever met."

Lenora drove south for about three quarters of an hour then turned west into the hills. A short drive later she turned onto a dirt road then approached a cabin set well back from the road. She stopped and let Roscoe out to pee then walked towards the cabin with him close on her heels. There was an older woman hanging out her wash on a line. "Good morning."

"Mornin'." The woman paused in her work to gaze at Lenora. "What's a city gal doin' way out here?"

Lenora took a cursory look around before returning her attention to the woman. "Looking for Billy Franks."

"What? My useless nephew? What's he done now?"

"Jumped bail."

"So, you gonna arrest him all by yourself?"

"I'm not a cop. I'm just here to take him back. That's how I get paid."

"Little gal, you a bounty hunter?"

"Yep, that I am."

"You're a goddam fool, is what you are, bitch." There was a big angry man standing in the doorway, a shotgun in his hands. "I'll bury you in the back forty with the rest."

"So, does this mean you won't come peaceably?"

For an answer he pulled the trigger, but Lenora had already shifted onto combat mode. She was behind him, driving her foot into the back of his knee then planting her other foot into the middle of his back. Billy Franks lay face down in the dirt, stunned, while she tied his hands behind him with the dog's leash. The old woman's jaw hung open as she watched the slim girl haul the huge man over to her car then stuff him in the trunk.

Lenora held the car door open and the dog jumped in. "Great day for drying the wash," she called, as she settled into the car then turned it around and drove away.

It was early afternoon when Billy Franks was herded into the police station by a woman carrying a shotgun. The policeman's jaw dropped when he saw her and who she had. "Afternoon, Officer." She passed him the shotgun. "I was talking to a nice lady when this man appeared and fired this shotgun at me. I disarmed him and brought him in. Is this man Billy Franks?"

"Yes, ma'am, it is indeed Billy Franks. Nice to see you again, Billy."

"Fuck you."

"You just wait right here, ma'am, while I tuck old Billy into a cell back here."

"I'll need my dog's leash back."

"You bet. You wait right there, and I'll get you a receipt for this fella." He returned in a moment then handed her back the leash. "I'll need a statement too."

"Sure. I located Billy Franks at his aunt's house. I asked him to come quietly, but he shot at me. I disarmed him, tied him up, tossed him in the trunk, and brought him back here as agreed."

"You disarmed him all by yourself?"

"I did, yes. I'm psychic, remember? I knew when he was going to fire, so I was already moving before he pulled the trigger. I got behind him. The rest was easy. Hardest part was getting that big heifer into the car."

"I'll just bet it was." The officer chuckled as he wrote out the receipt. "So, who do I make this receipt out to?"

"Lady Seeker."

"I'll need a real name."

"Lenora Jonson." She spelled it for him then asked directions to Mr. Gluagar's office.

"Holy shit, this is real," exclaimed Morty. "You actually brought in Billy Franks?"

"I did, yes. Now about that payment."

"Well, I didn't ..." He got no further as she leaned across the desk, almost nose to nose with him. "Wait, wait, I'll pay you. Jesus woman, settle down. I just didn't believe you could actually find him, let alone bring him in all by yourself."

"I'm tougher than I look." She straightened up again and stepped back. "Let me make this absolutely clear, Mr. Gluagar. I do the job, and then I get paid. That's how it works."

"And I have no problem with that. I don't."

"You just didn't believe I could do it?"

"No, I didn't. Look, just settle down here with a cup of coffee and I'll go get your money." She nodded and sank into a chair. "Sorry about getting bitchy. I'm over tired, hungry, been shot at, and it's that time of the month."

"No harm done. Look, Seeker, I've got a couple more if you want 'em."

"Sure. I'll take a look when you get back."

He nodded and stepped out the office door. Lenora sighed and poured herself a coffee. She took a sip and made a face then sighed and added more sugar before taking a second sip. It didn't help much. She sank back into a chair to wait. A short while later he returned. Opening his briefcase, he counted out the money and passed it to her.

"Thanks, Mr. Gluagar."

"Morty, call me Morty."

"You can call me Seeker. You had a couple more for me to look at?"

"Sure, just a minute while I find the files here." He rummaged around on his desk for a moment then passed her two files.

"Morty."

"Yes?"

"You make terrible coffee."

"No shit." He chuckled. "So, can you do anything with those?"

"What's the story on this woman?"

"Abused wife, killed her husband. She jumped bail about six weeks ago."

"That's self defense, I won't hunt her. What about this guy?"

"Custody dispute. Stole the kids and ran, but they caught him in Florida and sent him back. He jumped bail about three months ago. Cost me a fortune, the bastard."

"Okay, give me a minute. She closed her eyes then began to whisper the man's name, calling to him. She finally settled on a location. "This'll take me a few days. What's the bounty?"

"Eight thousand."

"Plus expenses?"

"Expenses? Are you kidding me? I can't afford to pay expenses. Jesus woman."

"Come on, Morty, two hundred fifty a day for gas, food, and lodgings. Besides I have to feed him when I bring him back."

"Bringing him back. Girl, that's usually where people run into trouble. Sometimes they manage to bring him back, sometimes they don't. You know what I mean? It's when you get tired they can get you."

"Okay, good to know. I still need gas and lodgings. Come on, Morty. Two fifty a day. What do you say?"

He grinned as he shook his head. "You're selling yourself short, Seeker. Those other bums charge me three hundred a day for expenses. Okay, eight thou plus three hundred a day. Is it a deal?"

"Deal," she replied, offering to shake on it.

He shook her hand then spoke. "I'll get you the paperwork for this guy. You need that when you turn him in."

"Paperwork?"

"A copy of the bond he signed and the bail piece."

"Bail piece?"

"Proof that he's a fugitive."

"Okay, got it."

"You're pretty new at this, aren't you?"

"Today's my first day."

"You're joking. Who're your partners? They should have told you all this stuff."

"No partners, Morty. Just me and my dog."

"Tougher than you look, girl. Look, here's three days extra expenses to get you going."

"Thanks, Morty. See you in a few days." She took her money and walked out.

Lenora got back into her car and headed out of town, going north. She stopped at a fast food joint to fill her belly then continued on her way. She had a long drive ahead of her.

Later she and Roscoe spent the night in a motel. "You know what, Roscoe? When we get paid for this next job we should trade the old car in for a used camper van. You know, something a bit more comfortable for a couple of nomads like us." Roscoe just wagged his tail then brought her the tug-o-war toy.

"Oh yeah, so, it's like that is it?" He wagged his tail harder as she grabbed the end of the toy.

They drove north all the next day then spent another night in a motel. Early on the third day she located her quarry. He was in a cafe having coffee with a group of others. Two cops were also in the cafe. Lenora bought herself a coffee then went and sat with the man and his friends.

Her quarry leaned towards her and gave her an appreciative smile. "Well, now, just who are you, Delicious?"

"Hi, I'm Lennie. Are you Jason Eberly?"

At the sound of that name he leaped to his feet to run but she caught him by the shirt and hauled him to the floor, face down. She was kneeling on his back, twisting his arm behind him. "Whoa there, Sugar, don't run away again. Hold still now, I got ya."

"What the hell is going on here?" demanded one policeman, training his gun on her. "Back off. Back off now and get down on the floor."

Lenora spread her hands wide as she moved aside. "Easy, boys, don't let my prisoner escape."

"Your prisoner? Are you a cop?"

"Bounty hunter. This man's a bail jumper. I have his paperwork in my jacket pocket."

"Nice and easy, girl," said the second cop as she slowly, carefully, opened her jacket, pulled out the papers and handed them to him. He looked them over then offered her a hand up. "It's legit, Bill. Dirty bugger was right under our noses. She got him fair and square."

At that point the man broke free and bolted through the door. He was barely halfway across the parking lot when she tackled him from behind. "Damn, girl. You're sure fast," puffed the big policeman as they reached the two combatants. The man was trying to punch Lenora and she was holding back because of the police.

"Get up, you," said one policeman as he hauled the man to his feet.

"Hey, hey, hey, he's mine, I caught him both times."

"Relax, bounty hunter. You'll get your money. We're all going to take a ride to the station together. You'll get your man there and we'll take your statement."

Lenora nodded and dusted off her jeans. "Fair enough." Later that afternoon, fugitive in hand, she called Morty and reported in.

They'd been on the road for about an hour when her prisoner broke the silence. "How'd you find me?"

"I'm gifted. It's what I do, find people, things."

"I'm innocent, you know. My ex lied about me, and they stole my kids. There's no justice in the system, not for me."

"Could be true, my friend, but it's not my problem. My problem is making sure Roscoe and I have a roof over our heads and food in our bellies. This isn't personal, it's just a job."

"Yeah, I get that. Any chance for a washroom break? I'm busting back here."

"Sure, I could use a pee break myself. Next gas station."

A few minutes later she pulled off the highway and into a small town, located the gas station and pulled up to the pump. She pumped the gas then moved the car ahead before going in to pay. She took him with her. "So, are you going to hold the equipment or are you going to until my hands?"

"I'll untie you, but before I do, let me make this plain. I can outrun you, outfight you, and I'm quite willing to make you ride the rest of the way back in the trunk. Try anything stupid and you go in the trunk."

She untied his hands then he hit her hard and ran. He didn't even make it out of the parking lot before she had him. Lenora knocked him down then yanked him back to his feet. "Warned you, Asshole." She pushed him towards the building.

As she shoved him through the door he began to plead with the older woman working there. "Help me, please. Call the police. This woman is crazy, she'll kill me."

The woman looked terrified for a moment. Lenora grinned and winked at her. "Washrooms?" The woman pointed. "Oh, you can call the police if you want. This man is a fugitive from justice and my prisoner. I have all the paperwork with me so I can show that to the police."

"You a bounty hunter, girl?"

"Yes indeed."

"Good for you. What did he do?"

"Deadbeat dad and bail jumper. Get in there, you. If you're not back in five minutes I'll come in there and haul you out." She pushed him through the door and waited for it to close. Lenora then turned back to the woman and paid for her gas. "Is there a window in there he could crawl out of?" The woman nodded. Lenora grinned and slipped out the door.

He skinned his arm and belly as he struggled out the high window to land in a heap on the ground. He leaped to his feet and she caught the front of his shirt, spun him around, and pushed him towards the car. Spinning around, he lashed out and punched her in the mouth. Instinctively, she yelped and shrank away.

The man raced away into an open field but she caught him easily and knocked him face down in the dirt. She twisted his arm painfully behind him in a hammer lock. He howled as she brought him to his feet. "You crossed the line that time, buddy. Nobody hits me and gets away with it, not anymore. I gave you every chance to make this easy, but you wouldn't have it. Now you go in the trunk." He shouted and swore in protest, making vile threats, but it was no use.

Lenora went back inside after stuffing him in the trunk. She went to the washroom took care of business, then sighed as she cleaned herself up. She now had a fat lip and wasn't happy. She returned to the counter. "Don't suppose you folks sell rope, do you?"

The woman smiled and pulled a fifty-foot length of thin rope off the wall. "Now, let me show you a trick, girl." She pulled the wrapper off the rope and pulled off a length. She cut it then turned to Lenora. "Watch carefully now. This is what they used to do in the old west when they didn't have handcuffs." She showed Lenora how to wind the rope with two long tails and two loops. "Stick out your hands."

Lenora did and the woman slipped the rope cuffs on her and pulled them tight. "Now you tie the ends behind his back, like this," she went on. "See, no dang way a man could get out of that." Lenora struggled for a minute then smiled. The woman loosened the rope cuffs so Lenora could get out then she shook out the loops. "Now, you try it."

A few more minutes of instruction and Lenora could tie the knots. Smiling with delight she thanked the woman, paid for the rope, and returned to her car. There were two men trying to rescue the shouting man in the trunk. "Hey, get away from my prisoner."

"Prisoner?" Both men turned to face Lenora.

"You leave that bounty hunter gal alone, Tommy." The gas station attendant had come out to see what the fuss was. "She's got a dangerous man in there."

"Oh, sorry ma'am." They backed away from the car. "We thought the guy was just stuck in there."

"Yeah, he's a real con man, this guy. No harm done." She unlocked the trunk then hauled him to his feet. "Stick out your hands." Reluctantly, he complied. She tied the rope cuffs on him then stuffed him in the back seat. She waved to her new friend as she drove away.

"You stupid fucking bitch, I'll kill you for this. You've got to sleep sometime and when you do ..."

Lenora's patience snapped. "What the hell is the matter with you? Can't you learn? You've tried me several times and I beat you every time.

Now sit there and shut the hell up or I'll put you back in the trunk with a gag in your mouth."

"I'm gonna sue your stupid ass."

"Whine, whine, whine. Jesus, no wonder that woman sent you packing. I wouldn't want you anywhere near kids either. Now, I've got a mouth gag shaped like a penis. I hear one more sound from you and you'll have that in your mouth for the rest of the ride." He shut up. He didn't know if she was bluffing or not, but he wasn't willing to chance it.

Lenora drove through the night and arrived at the police station just before noon the next day. As she entered the building, herding her prisoner ahead of her, there was a ruckus going on. A man, woman, and a policeman were trying to subdue a big man who was going wild. He was knocking them around and trying to get to the door even though his hands were cuffed.

Without a second thought Lenora hopped on the man's back, wrapping her arms around his head and neck. Powerful legs squeezed his chest and strong arms squeezed tightly. He struggled wildly for a moment then slowly began to fall. When he was lying still on the floor Lenora pushed him away. "My god, you killed him," said the woman.

"He's fine, it's a sleeper hold. He'll have a wicked headache when he wakes up, but he's fine."

"Hey, Seeker," said the policeman, "your prisoner just ran for it."

"That dirty son of a bitch." Lenora snarled as she ran from the building. In a heartbeat she had his scent and gave chase. It took her mere moments to run him to ground. She locked the sleeper on him then threw him over her shoulder and carried him back to the police station.

She dropped him in a chair and slapped his face a few times to bring him around. She passed over the paperwork and waited until her prisoner was locked away. She thanked the officer for the receipt then turned away.

Lenora parked in front of Morty's office, clipped Roscoe onto a leash, then went inside. The couple from the police station were there talking to Morty. "Hey, there she is now. Seeker, this is Jane and Carl Billings. Jane was just telling me how you put the sleeper on Big Max Durl."

"Yeah, it's a handy hold. Hi folks, nice to meet 'cha."

"You too, Lady Seeker," replied Carl. "Morty says you're stealing all our work."

"Oh?"

"Relax, Seeker," said Jane. "We make a swing by here about once a month, but we've been busy lately."

"Sorry guys, didn't mean to horn in on anybody's territory, but starvation sucks."

"Indeed it does," replied Jane. "So, Seeker, Morty says you're tougher than you look."

"Yeah." Lenora passed her receipt over to Morty. "I get that a lot." She watched carefully as Morty counted out her money. "Thanks, Morty. Got any more?"

"Just the one you didn't want."

"That's okay, I need a few days off anyway. I want to trade my old car for a camper van or some such thing. Me and Roscoe need a home."

"So, you've got a fella working with ya?" asked Carl.

"Roscoe here is my main man. He's a great tracker and he doesn't give me any stress about where I hang my undies to dry." Everybody had a good laugh at that.

"Would you consider teaming up with us for a job?" asked Jane.

"One job? Yeah, I guess I could do that. I need a couple of days sleep first, though. Once I catch up on sleep and trade in the car I'll be good to go. Who's the target?"

"Fella named Wooten out of Austin Texas. He's a bad man and carries lots of guns. We'd have better chances with three of us."

"You guys got the paperwork on him?"

"Sure do."

"All right, what's the money?"

"Three way split," said Carl.

Lenora sighed and tucked her pay into the shoulder bag she was carrying. "Give me numbers I can understand, Carl."

"Forty-five hundred to you."

"Sorry." She started to walk away. She grinned as she saw Jane slap Carl hard on the shoulder.

"All right, the reward for him is thirty thousand. Ten for you."

Lenora winked at Jane. "I'll sleep on it." She opened the door and Roscoe darted through. They watched her go.

"Well, people, I'd say your chances of survival just went from zero to you might just make it," said Morty.

"She truly that good, Morty?"

"She is, Carl. Billy Franks had a shotgun and she brought him in in the trunk of her car. Yeah, I'd say she's pretty good."

Jane grinned. "Looks like we'll be staying in town a few days."

"IT DOESN'T LOOK LIKE much, but my Bill was a mechanic. He retired two years ago, but cancer took him last year. We never did go camping in it." The older woman looked sad as she and Lenora inspected the camper van. "It's an older model, but Bill worked on it for years. Listen to the engine purr." She started the engine and, true to her word, it fairly purred. The interior was perfect as well. A man's dream to be bought for a few thousand dollars.

Lenora smiled as she looked the van over. "Ma'am, you're asking far too little for this. It's worth a lot more."

"Maybe, but not if you can't sell it. And I have tried. The medical expenses for Bill ruined us. Our savings are gone and all I have left is the house. I'll soon have to sell that and move in with my daughter."

"I'm so sorry to hear that. Okay, I'll buy this, but only if you'll let me pay double for it."

"What? Are you crazy? What's wrong with your head, girl?"

Lenora smiled brightly. "Not a dang thing. That's my offer, take it or leave it."

The woman suddenly stepped into Lenora's arms and hugged her tightly. "Thank you," she whispered as she continued her hug. "God bless your loving heart. This will make a big difference to me. I'll be able to keep the house another year with this." She released Lenora and stepped back. "Maybe I can even turn the place into a B&B and make a living that way."

Lenora opened her shoulder bag and began to count out the money. "I'll be a regular customer when I'm in town."

"My god, child, you carry that kind of cash around with you?"

"Not usually, however, I just got paid for a couple of jobs. I get paid in cash because I don't trust banks."

"Right."

Lenora heard the change in the woman's tone and looked up to see fear written on the woman's face. "Hey, I'm not a drug dealer or anything, I'm a bounty hunter. I've been working for Mr. Morton Gluagar. You can check me out with him and the police. The call me Lady Seeker."

"You're serious."

"I am."

"They call you Seeker?"

"Yep, but my name is Lenora. Call me Lennie."

"All right, Lennie. I'm Mary Jo to my friends."

"A pleasure to make your acquaintance, Mary Jo. Here's your money."

"And here's your pink slip."

"Thank you. Now, I have another question for you. Since that garage will now be empty, would you rent it out?"

"What? Sure, I guess so. I had to sell my car last year to pay the taxes, so I have no real use for it. Why?"

"Well, I can't drive both vehicles at the same time, and since you won't take my old car in trade, I'll need a place to keep whichever one I'm not using. How about a hundred a month?"

The woman just gazed at Lenora. "What are you doing, child?"

"Paying it forward, Mary Jo. Please let me."

"Oh child, that had a lot of pain in it."

"I was down, broken, bleeding out, couldn't breathe, fading fast. Someone saved me, sent me to people who helped me get myself right, and then they told me to pay it forward when the time came. This seemed like the right time to me. Now, here's a year's rent on the garage in advance. You might as well use the car when I'm gone as I'll be using the camper most of the time. You'll have to buy your own gas, though. I'm not running a charity here."

"The hell you're not." Mary Jo hugged the younger woman tightly again.

"Listen you, I'm the big scary bounty hunter. Don't you tell a living soul about this, or I'll be ruined. Now, get your purse and hop in the camper with me and Roscoe. I want to take her for a test drive, so we'll give you an escort to the bank with all that cash."

Lenora drove into town and parked near the door of the bank. She smiled as she watched Mary Jo go inside. "Lady Moragah?"

"I am here, Lady Seeker."

"Did I do wrong here?"

"No, you did right, my daughter. Sometimes you can defend the weak without violence. This is a good woman, and you can trust her. You have defended her against a cold unfeeling system, and it brought no harm to anyone to do it. I'm quite proud of you, Lenora."

"I'm not being a wimp here, am I?"

"No, you are being a priestess of Moragah, you are defending the weak, helping a person in need."

"Lady Moragah, are you ever going to tell me what it is you made me to find?"

"*First I made you to find yourself. One day soon we will discuss the other, but events have transpired to give us more time. Be at peace, my daughter. All is unfolding as it should.*"

"Thank you, mother goddess. I did need the reassurance."

Moragah sent a wave of warm loving energy through Lenora then gently pulled back. Mary Jo was returning. "So, everything all right?"

"Perfect," replied the older woman. "They wanted to know where I got all the cash. I said I found it in one of Bill's old tool chests in the garage."

"Oh?"

"Yes, well, it's none of their damn business where I got it, is it? Everything is legal and none of their business."

"Damn straight, so, should we go shopping while we're in town?"

"Oh lord, yes. I haven't been shopping in forever."

A Hard Capture

The next morning, Lenora climbed out of the camper with Roscoe and headed out for a wild run through a piece of the city. She'd left the camper van in the parking lot of the city park. Once Roscoe was tuckered out she fed him, and then left him guarding the camper while she climbed easily up to the roof tops for a serious workout. She was tired and happy as she returned to the van.

With a bit of effort she managed to get the tiny shower going and enjoyed getting cleaned up. A short time later found her at a laundromat. Jane and Carl were there as she came in. "Hey there, Lady Seeker," said Carl. "You ready to go to work yet?"

"Hi Carl, Jane. Yep, just got a few errands to finish then we can get together and start work."

Jane smiled as she continued folding her laundry. "How about noon, at Morty's office?"

"Works for me. I'll bring Roscoe along. He's a great tracker, but you can pay him with hot dogs."

"Roscoe, that's your beagle, right? I'll bring him a better treat than a hot dog."

Lenora smiled to herself as she finished her laundry then went about buying the few groceries and dog food she'd need to fill her few small cupboards. She grabbed a burger at a drive through then returned to Morty's office. Carl and Jane were waiting there for her.

"Hi guys, sorry I'm late."

"No worries," replied Carl. "You finally ready?"

"Maybe. Let's see the paperwork on this guy." Carl passed it over. "Jonas Lamonde. So, where are you, Jonas? Talk to me now, where are you?"

"I told you, he's in Austin Texas."

"No he isn't, Carl. Hush now, let me work. Come on, Jonas, talk to me. Where are you? Where are you. So there you are. Okay, let me, ... oh shit. Damnit, he's in North Bay."

"Are you serious? That's barely a day's drive from here," said Jane.

"I'm serious, but that changes things."

"What do you mean?" asked Carl.

"He's with a gang of men, all with guns, but we knew that was a possibility," replied Lenora. "However, it's the city that's the problem."

"Why is that a problem?"

"It's a problem because I know who else is there, and I don't want to mess with her territory. Listen, I like you guys, so here's the new deal. I'll make contact with some special people there. If they're okay with it, I'll bring him out and hand him over to you to turn in."

"Wait, wait, just hang on a minute," said Carl. "What the hell is going on here? Who the hell is in North Bay and why does that change things?"

Lenora sighed and seemed to phase out for a moment. "Lady Moragah, can I truly trust these folks?" she asked silently.

"These are honest people, Lenora. You can trust them, but I wouldn't let them know about Lady Shadow."

"Okay guys, tell me straight. Are you truly hellbent on bringing this man in?"

"You damn right we are," replied Carl. "Tell me what just scared the crap out of you and why you don't want to go to North Bay?"

"Ever heard of the Viper?"

"What, the scary guy in shiny armor with snakes painted on his face? They say he's death on street gangs. Why?"

"He's in North Bay right now. People, if we get in his way we're nothing more than collateral damage. The Viper will wipe out the gang and us with it. Won't bother him at all."

"The Viper? Jesus, girl, you know that maniac?" asked Morty.

"I've never met him in person, Morty, but I know enough to stay well out of his way. The thing is, he's not the scariest thing in town. We need to be very careful if we go there."

"We're always careful," replied Jane.

"Jane, think this over," said Morty. "I didn't believe anything could scare Seeker. After all, she faced Billy Franks and he had a shotgun. She brought him back in the trunk of her car. If Seeker doesn't want to go after this guy, maybe you should think it over."

Suddenly Lenora sank to the floor in a cross-legged position and seemed to phase out. In actuality she was in a forest glade talking to a tall red haired elf who had a dragon peeking over her shoulder. *"Talk to each other, my children."*

"Hey there, Dragon Rider." Lenora's nervousness showing.

"Do not fear me so, my sister. I will never bring you harm. Come closer to me, Aeroth wants to meet you."

Lenora swallowed hard and stepped closer. The dragon stretched out his neck and sniffed her. A purring gurgle came from deep in his throat as he rubbed his head against her. "He likes you, Lenora. I don't mean to frighten you, my sister. I don't."

"I know. I can feel you now and you feel good, like Penny. She said I'd like you and she was right. It's just that you're so much more powerful than me, and in the past that's always meant pain."

"I understand, girl, but know this. I nearly got myself killed a couple of times trying to track down a bad guy. If I'd had you to help me, it would have saved me a lot of pain. Lenora, I'm just a girl like you, trying to figure out how this all works."

Lenora was rubbing Aeroth behind his eye ridges now and he snuggled closer to her. "Lady Shadow, is it okay if I come into your city to make a bust?"

"You may call me Seline. Just a moment." The elf woman morphed into a girl and grinned. "Sorry, I tend to be a bit formal in elf mode. Penny said you'd get here sooner or later. You want some help?"

"I've got partners for this job. I'd like to keep them alive. This man is dangerous. That part doesn't scare me. However, he's involved with a gang, and I don't want my people to get caught in the middle if Viper goes after the gang before we make our bust."

"Got it. Who's your target?"

"Man named Jonas Lamonde."

"Okay, got it. I'll see what we can dig up on this guy before you get here. I'll talk to Vic and make sure he knows you're coming. Show me your people now." Lenora thought of Carl and Jane for a moment then Seline smiled. "Okay, got it. Lenora, if you need any help, call me. Promise me now."

"Lennie, my friends call me Lennie. I promise, Seline."

The vision faded and Lenora opened her eyes. She rose with liquid grace and nodded at Carl. "Okay, we go in together. I know where he is, and we'll be okay."

"What did you just do?" asked Jane, her voice hushed.

"I just talked to the most dangerous person on this planet, told her we're coming. She gave me the go ahead. She'll let Viper know to stay back until we have our guy. Saddle up, I want to get this done."

IT WAS JUST AFTER MIDNIGHT when they pulled up in Carl's truck. They parked a few houses away from the target then slipped out into the darkened streets. "Okay, that's the house."

"You sure?" asked Carl.

"Absolutely sure. Now, look carefully down the street. You can just make out the car in the shadows. See it?"

Carl gazed into the gloom for a moment. "Yeah, I see it. Holy shit, that's a Viper. Oh god, is that his car? Is he there?"

"Yeah, it's his car and he's here somewhere, watching. Now here's how we do this. Jane, you watch the front door and Carl, you watch the back in case our boy makes a run for it."

"Okay, so where will you be?"

"I'm going in after him."

"Alone?"

"Just get in position." Lenora turned away from them and ran to the house. With a mighty leap she gained the porch roof then was in through an upstairs window. Carl and Jane raced to get in position.

A woman had seen her enter but had no time to scream before Lenora grabbed her in the sleeper hold. She dropped the unconscious body to the floor and slipped out of the bedroom and into the hallway. She could hear the men laughing and drinking in the living room downstairs. A quick glimpse told her there were guns everywhere, and about seven men. A second glimpse gave her the man she wanted. He was over next to the wall by the fireplace.

The party broke up suddenly as a whirlwind landed in their midst. Bodies and weapons flew everywhere then Jonas Lamonde had his arm twisted behind his back and steely fingers gripped his throat. "All right, boys," came a woman's cold deadly voice. "Before you start shooting, know this. Jonas is the one I want. Make a hole for me to take him out and nobody gets hurt."

"Sure, bitch. And if we don't?"

"Viper is waiting outside for me to come out. If I scream he'll come in. If I go out he'll wait until I'm clear. That's all the time you have. Your call."

"Oh fuck this ..." The man went for his gun, but there was no time. Lenora dropped her man and moved. The man reaching for the gun died instantly as her boot connected with his skull. His gun was suddenly in her hand and the others started to fall.

Jonas made a run for it, but bolted through the door and into the baseball bat Carl swung at him, catching him in the belly. The gunfire inside stopped, and Carl had Jonas down. Suddenly a big man in armor ran past them and into the house. Lenora came out and tossed aside the empty gun. A moment later Viper reappeared.

Carl and Jane were very quiet as the Viper stooped and scooped up the gun Lenora had tossed aside. The man was big, and, even in that metallic armor, he moved easily, like a hunting cat. There was no face, just a metal visor with a cobra painted on it. "Is this the only gun you touched?" That voice was deep, cold, unfeeling.

"Yes," replied Lenora.

"I'll dispose of it for you. Next time wear gloves." He stood still as a statue for a moment then held his huge fist out towards her. "Good job in there." She gave him a fist bump and he stalked away. A moment later they heard the scream of the tires as he sped down the empty street.

Lenora sighed and gestured to the man on the ground. "Come on, let's load this guy up and get out of here."

Her partners agreed. Carl hauled Jonas to his feet and stuffed him, now in cuffs and leg irons, into the back seat of the truck. He climbed behind the wheel and Jane scooted in beside him. Lenora got in beside the door. "What happened in there, Seeker?" asked Carl.

"I had our guy under control, using him as a shield. I told those guys Viper was outside, gave them a chance to run. It's just like my sister says, they never have enough sense to lay down the guns and walk away."

"You stupid bitch, my brothers will know what went down here. They'll find you and you'll wish you were dead long before they make it happen."

Lenora turned in her seat. "Jonas, I have a gag in my purse. It's shaped like a penis, and if I hear another word out of your mouth you'll be sucking on that all the way home. Now shut the hell up." Carl chuckled at that, but there was only silence from the back seat.

They reached her camper and parked. "Okay, guys, are you sure you can get this guy back in one piece?"

"No problem, Seeker," replied Jane. "You okay?"

"I'm a little bummed out."

"Viper said you did a good job in there. That was you shooting?"

"Yeah, it was. I had Jonas and offered them a chance to walk away, but they went for the guns instead."

"One guy went for a gun, bitch. You killed them all," said the voice from the back seat.

Lenora's eyes bored into his. "I don't play around, asshole. I've been hurt too bad too often to give jerks like you many chances. Nobody moved towards a door, everybody went for a gun. Yes, I killed them, and if you had a dead or alive poster on you I'd have killed you, too. Know this, you send people after me, they go down hard and fast. I don't play, not ever. They come at me they don't go home.

"Carl, you watch this moron."

"I will, Seeker. Sure you don't want to come with us?"

"No, now I have to go back into the city and pay my respects. We got special treatment tonight."

"What did this cost you, Seeker?" There was genuine concern in Jane's voice.

"More than you might guess. Be careful folks. You can send my share care of Morty." She shut the door then stepped back from the truck and watched until it was out of sight. Roscoe was barking so she opened the camper and let him out. He ran to the nearest tree then lifted a leg with a sigh of relief.

When he was done she clipped the leash on him then they went for a run. When they got back she gave him a treat then settled down on her bed. A few deep breaths and she had a visual of Seline. A heartbeat later Seline's eyes found her. She smiled and held up her finger. A moment later she seemed to materialize beside Lenora. "Hey there, everything go okay?"

"Yeah, more or less. Are you real or a vision?"

"Illusion, and it's tough to project so far, but I need the practice. Lenora, Vic is known for such actions as tonight's. He'll claim this one and nothing will come back at you."

"I owe you one, my sister. Anytime you need a seeker, I'm your gal."

"Awesome. Coming to visit?"

"I think I need a bit of alone time."

"This your first time having to kill someone?"

"Nope, Penny and I had a few battles in New York. It just doesn't get any easier."

"I know. And that, dear sister, is what really separates us from the bad guys. Are you sure you'll be okay?"

"Yeah, I'm okay."

"Sorry, don't believe you, but I'll leave you to it if you promise to call me the instant you change your mind."

"I promise. Seline."

"Yes?"

"Thanks."

The illusion smiled then vanished. "You know, Roscoe, I'm really starting to like that girl. She is just like me. I guess we all are, aren't we, Lady Moragah."

"Yes, my daughter, all my priestesses were broken when I made them. But you were all strong inside as well. Be at peace about what has happened, my child. Death is not the end of the spirit's existence, merely another path on the journey."

"Thank you, Lady. I guess I'm a bit messed up because I thought I'd be finding lost children, and stuff like that, not bringing in crazed killers."

"You may do as you wish, Lenora. You chose this path. If it doesn't meet your needs you may choose another. However, think about what

you have done so far. You reunited that woman with her daughter, saved the daughter from death by exposure, you returned three fugitives and provided for your own needs. Consider this, by removing those violent men from the streets, how many innocent women have you kept from harm?"

"Yeah, I hadn't thought of it like that. I wish Viper didn't have to take the blame for what I did, though. I suppose, even if I went in to confess they still wouldn't believe a girl could do that, especially when Viper was seen in the area. That's why he squealed his tires when he left, wasn't it."

"Yes it was. Victor and Seline both believe it will be helpful to all if you remain free of police scrutiny."

"So, I have to let the big kids protect me?"

"They're enjoying it, Lenora. Truly they are."

Lenora felt Moragah's amusement. "Okay, I'll stop sulking and let them baby me. I'm just afraid I might enjoy it too much."

"Lenora, what would Penny say about the way you're feeling right now?"

"She'd say I'm having a carbohydrate drop and need to eat something. Yeah, I guess I did run a lot of adrenaline tonight. Okay, I'll eat, then get some sleep."

"Be at peace, my daughter. I will protect your rest this night."

Lenora ate a bowl of cereal with raisins then crawled into the bed. The dog hopped up and snuggled in beside her. She gently stroked his head and smiled. "You know, Roscoe, as crazy as our lives have become, we're way ahead of where we were before, right?" For an answer he rolled onto his back and presented his belly for scratching.

Going Home

The sun was barely up, but Lenora suddenly awakened. Someone was outside the camper. She swiftly pulled on shorts and a top then opened the door. "All right, whoever you are, you're about to get your ass kicked."

"Aw come on, girl. I just came to buy you breakfast." Seline was standing beside a shiny Mercedes, a bright smile on her face.

Lenora sighed and shook her head. "Oh gods, you're a morning person, aren't you?"

"Never used to be, but Ellen has me converted."

"Ellen, your partner?"

"That's right, my sweetie and the real brains of the outfit. She and Debbie are slaving away at the computer right now, so I sneaked away. Come on, hop in. Bring your boyfriend."

"Okay. Come on, Roscoe. The pretty lady wants to buy you breakfast." She got in the car with Roscoe in her lap. "We going to a restaurant?"

"Yup."

"Can we leave the car running with the AC on for my buddy? Day's gonna be hot."

"We'll bring him with us."

"Cool. A restaurant that allows dogs. How do they get that past the health authorities?"

"This is one of those new places. You probably haven't heard of them yet. They call them sidewalk cafes."

Lenora groaned and sank deeper into the plush seat. "Seline, if you tease me again before I have coffee, I swear I'll ..."

"Whoa there, super sister, easy girl. Just hold that threat until we get your caffeine levels back up. Okay, here we are and they're just opening. Perfect."

The young waiter was just setting up the tables as the big car opened up and two pretty girls got out. They had his full attention. Seline called out to him. "Hey there, coffee for two and lots of it, then bring the menus." He grinned and went back inside. By the time she'd locked up the car and they walked around the barrier to the seating area, he was back with the coffee and menus. Lenora moaned softly as she took her first long sip from the cup. Seline ordered breakfast and extra sausages for Roscoe.

Once the food arrived and Lenora had her second cup of coffee finished, Seline smiled and leaned back in her chair. "So, feeling better?"

"Much. Seline, I can't thank you enough for this."

"All my pleasure."

"So, why did you come?"

"After we talked last night, I discussed it with Ellen. Hope that's okay."

"Sure, no problem at all. What was her take on it?"

"She pointed out that all Moragah's priestesses were broken when she made them. Ellen thinks there's more going on for you than you've said."

"And you just can't leave it alone, right?"

Seline smiled. "I will if you say so, but I get the impression you need to talk. Besides, Moragah herself told us to talk to each other. That tells me a lot is at stake here."

"It's okay, girl. I'm not afraid of you anymore. We're good here."

"I can still feel you're hurting."

"And you won't let it go?"

"Nope. Talk to me."

Lenora refilled the coffee cup from the pot the waiter had brought. She stirred it thoughtfully with one hand while scratching Roscoe behind the ear with the other. "Okay. When Moragah found me I was lying in a pool of my own blood, in the driveway of my father's house."

"Your father's house, not your home."

"My father is a violent, controlling man. He beat my mother and me as long as I can remember. This time I was done, dying. If Moragah hadn't healed me I'd have ended my short life right there in the driveway, at his hands."

"And that's what you're really afraid of now, that you'll become like him."

Lenora sighed and gazed down at Roscoe. "Yeah, pretty much. Yes, at first you scared me. You're the only one who knows and can see me when I'm searching for them. That scared the crap out of me."

"And now?"

"We're good, Seline. No, it was last night when I took those guys down. I didn't think about it, I just killed them, like it was no big deal at all."

"Did you enjoy it?"

"What? No!"

"Were you angry?"

"No, no, not at all. I just knew it was them or me and I did what I had to do, but ..."

"No buts, sister. You're not like the bad guys because you took no pleasure in the killing, no thrill. You're not like your father because you weren't upset, angry, no rage pushing you, no uncontrolled passion. That is what he's like, isn't it?"

"Yeah, that's him all right, upset, angry, filled with blind rage."

"Then you're not like him, nor will you ever be."

"You sure about that?"

"One hundred per cent."

"Oh?"

"Honey, Moragah would never have given you extra abilities, made you a priestess, if there was any chance at all of you becoming like that."

"Yeah, I guess that makes sense."

"Hey, Goddess of Wisdom, Defender of the Weak, remember? Would a goddess who defends the weak create an aggressor?"

Lenora gave a gentle smile as she absorbed that argument. "No, I guess She wouldn't at that."

"Feeling better now?"

"Yes I am. Gods, this having big sisters thing is awesome. First she plies me with coffee then talks sense to me. Seline, thanks for not letting it go."

"My pleasure, now I want a favor."

"Sure. Name it."

"When you meet that grouchy dragon rider, don't take offense at her bossiness?"

"Done," replied Lenora, a bright smile on her lips at last. Seline's phone made a sound like a waterfall and she frowned at it. "Everything okay?"

"There's something going on. We've been hearing whispers on the street, rumblings through the grapevine. Something nasty, evil, is at work and we're trying to get a handle on whatever, or whoever, it is."

"Well, I just find stuff, people. Doubt I could be of much help there."

"It's okay, Sis. We're private detectives, this is what we do. Once we get a handle on this, I might ask you to help me pinpoint whoever is behind it."

"Any time, Seline. Any time at all."

"Deal." Seline looked up from the phone and smiled. "Sadly, it looks like I have to get to work. I'll take you, and your boyfriend there, back to the camper."

As Lenora got out and shut the car door, the window rolled down. "Hey, Seeker, check this out." Lenora clapped her hands in delight as the shiny car morphed into a battered old Ford with a gray haired man behind the wheel. She waved as the old car puttered off down the street.

"Sister Penny was right, Roscoe. Seline is a bubble of fun. I still wouldn't want to piss her off, though. So, how about we go for a run to burn off some of that breakfast?" Roscoe was in full agreement.

After the run Roscoe settled down for a nap while Lenora went for a wild free running session. She had fallen completely in love with Penny's favorite exercise program. A shower followed that, then she set out for home. Funny how that small city had already started to feel like home. Lenora was actually looking forward to seeing Morty and Mary Jo. She was halfway there where her senses went off like skyrockets.

"Shit." She fought the van to the side of the road. It took only a moment to home in on the cause of the problem. Hysterical parents and a missing child. In less than ten minutes she was in the driveway of a farmhouse, along with two police cars and the hysterical parents.

She hopped out of the van and approached the group, Roscoe right on her heels. "What's happened?"

"Who're you?" demanded a policeman.

"Our baby girl," sobbed the woman. "Someone took my baby girl."

"Ma'am, we haven't established that as yet. We ..."

"Show me a picture," said Lenora.

"Listen you, I want to see your ID," said the policeman as he grabbed her arm.

He was shocked at the power of her grip as she removed his hand. "Don't do this, not now. There's a child's life on the line. I can help, I can find her. I'm psychic, it's what I do."

"Here's her picture," said the father, passing Lenora a pic of a little girl with no front teeth and big brown eyes. "Her name's Katie."

Lenora gazed at the picture for a moment then began to slowly turn in a circle, talking softly. "Where are you, Katie? Where are you? Tell me where to find you. Ah, there you are. Okay, she's not far away, but she's tied up and in the trunk of a car. It's not moving right now. Shit, it's moving. Let's go."

"Hold it right there. Get down on the ground, now. Spread ..."

He got no further as Lenora was behind him with his own gun at his head. "There's no time for this. You can go all macho bullshit superman after we get the girl back, okay? Right now we have a child to find. Help me here. Keep a gun on me the whole time if you need to, but help me." She released him and gave him back his gun.

"Just who the hell are you?" He was sulky as he and the other police holstered their weapons.

"They call me Lady Seeker. I'm psychic." She closed her eyes for a moment. "Okay, car's stopped again. Ah, there you are, you son of a bitch. I'm coming for you. If that child's hurt you're a dead man."

"Seeker?" asked another of the police. "You're that bounty hunter from up state?"

"Yup, that's me. I need a map of this area."

"Got one right here." The second policeman whipped out a map and spread it out on the hood of his car.

Lenora looked at it closely for a moment. "Dammit, he's moving again. Okay, he's still in the city. He headed along this street. That's why the stops, traffic lights. He's headed for the highway."

"Can you tell what he looks like?" asked the policeman she disarmed.

"About thirty, five-eight, a hundred sixty pounds or so, brown hair, pale skin, thick glasses, heavy eyebrows, ..."

"Anything like this guy?" He showed her a picture.

"Yes. That's him. Moving again. Come on. One of you parents come with me. You too, Officer. I said you could keep me honest."

They hurried aboard the van, and Roscoe hopped into the young mother's lap. "Officer ..."

"Blaise. Officer Andy Blaise."

"I'm just Seeker. Okay, Officer Blaise, tell your friends to block him off but don't make a fuss. We don't want a high speed chase with that child in the trunk of his car. Tell one of them to lead me through traffic so I can get ahead of him."

Heart racing with the thrill and anticipation of the coming night, the young man fought to keep his speed down. He was safely away, mere blocks from the highway. It had been an easy snatch. Suddenly a woman with a dog on a leash stumbled in front of him. He slammed on the brakes to keep from hitting her. "Come on, Lady, move your ass." He shouted and swore as she sat on the street holding her ankle.

"I can't, I think it's broken. It's all your goddam fault. Why the hell can't you watch where you're going? You'll have to help me to the hospital."

"The hell I will." He snarled as he jerked the wheel hard, planning to go around her.

Suddenly a police car stopped right beside him, blocking him. He panicked and jumped from the car. He sprinted away, but the woman brought him down in less than half a block. He tried to kick and punch at her, but she grabbed him by the ear and dragged him back, howling in pain. She thrust him at the policeman. "Get her out of that trunk."

"Hey, hey, hey, you can't open my trunk. I don't give you permission to do that. You do that and anything you find can't be used against me in court."

"Oh for fuck sake. I'm not a cop so it won't matter what I do." She stepped to the back of the car, spun and lashed out. Her kick broke the lock, and the trunk lid flew open to reveal a child, bound and gagged. Lenora gently lifted her out and untied the gag in the girl's mouth. "Easy sweetie, easy. I've got you. Your momma is right around the corner. You wait here with the policemen, and I'll get her for you." She passed the girl to the arms of a policeman then returned to the van.

A moment later she was back with the child's mother. She smiled as the woman screamed the child's name and scooped her into her arms.

Lenora walked up to the policeman who'd tried to arrest her. "Okay, Officer Blaise, we did the deed. What now?"

The other officers were watching carefully. "All right, Bounty Hunter, we have outstanding issues here. There's the matter of resisting arrest, interfering with the police in their attempts to carry out their duties, and assaulting a police officer."

"Wow, sounds like I'm a serious badass."

"Actually, you are." His grin matched her own. "However, I think there may be a way out of this for you, since your intentions were noble, and it is your first offense."

"Oh? Do tell."

"The badly maligned officer in question might be persuaded to drop all charges in return for your company at dinner tonight."

"Oh really? That won't be construed as attempting to bribe an officer, will it?"

"Not if the officer pays."

"What about your wife, is she coming too?"

"She left me about six months ago, haven't heard from her since."

"I could find her for you, if you like."

"Please don't." That made her laugh, and his grin grew broader. "How about it, Seeker. Have dinner with me?"

"All right, as long as I can bring my boyfriend along."

"Boyfriend?"

"Roscoe."

"Deal. I know a place where they do great barbecue, we can eat outdoors, and Roscoe can chaperon. I get off shift in three hours. Where do I find you?"

"I have to drive Katie and her mom home. I could hang out there and help them tighten up their security until you get off shift." She turned to the mother. "Would that work for you?"

"Oh yes, of course. Please, come home with us. My husband will want to thank you in person."

She drove them home and stayed for a look around. In the end all she could recommend was getting a dog. "There's plenty of dogs in the shelters just begging for a home. See how Katie and Roscoe are getting along?" The traumatized child was fascinated with Roscoe, and he was more than willing to stay with his head in her lap.

They offered a reward, she refused, accepting only a few fresh garden vegetables for her tiny fridge. The off duty policeman arrived and she followed him to the restaurant in her van. There was music, beer, great food, and dancing. Lenora tried her best to be sociable, but he felt her hesitation. He gave up and walked her and Roscoe back to her van.

"Not lighting your fire, am I?" he asked, a rueful smile on his face.

"Sorry. I guess I'm just too much of a loner, and you're not ready."

"I talked about Jody too much, didn't I?"

"You've still got a thing there. You need to talk to her and get some closure."

"Actually, I'd like to, but I have no idea where the hell she is."

"Buffalo, she's in Buffalo."

"What? You sure?"

"Yep."

"That dirty lying old cow. Her mother swore she wasn't there. Thanks, Seeker. I guess I owe you one."

Lenora stepped into his arms, gave him a gentle hug, kiss on the cheek, then stepped away and opened the van door. "Take care of yourself, Andy." She and Roscoe climbed inside and drove away. He stood watching until she was out of sight.

The next day she pulled up in front of Morty's office. The first thing she saw as she entered was the new coffee maker. He looked up and grinned. "Go ahead, Seeker. You can't fail with this baby."

She made her selection, put in the cup, and hit the button. When it was ready she took a sip and groaned with delight. "Now that's coffee. What made you decide to upgrade?"

"I was getting too many complaints from the customers. Oh, speaking of customers, Carl wired the money to me for your bust. I've got it in the safe. Just be a minute." He disappeared into the back room and Lenora sank into a chair to enjoy her coffee.

"Here you go, Seeker. It's all there. You can count it if you like."

"I trust you, Morty. What's the matter with you? You're acting like I might bite you or something."

He sighed and sank into his chair behind the desk. "Sorry. It's just that I talked to Carl."

"Yeah, what did he say that has you so rattled?"

"He said you went into the house alone against an armed gang. Lots of screams and gunfire. The fugitive comes running out and Carl nabs him. A minute later you walk out, not a scratch. The Viper goes in to check, makes no sound then comes back and says you did a great job. Six dead, according to the police. Carl said the Viper took the blame for the hit, but it was you. He said to never piss you off."

"Carl talks too much. Morty ..."

"Easy, Seeker, easy. Carl will keep quiet, but he wanted to give me a heads up. What was said will stay within these walls. We're friends now, right?"

"Morty, I should kick your ass for even thinking I'd hurt you. The only thing saving you is this coffee." She smiled and he gave a nervous laugh. "Look, we are friends. I'll tell you more. I gave those guys the option of running away. Just drop the guns and walk away, but ..."

"You're just a girl and they had the guns?"

"Pretty much."

"So, why didn't you want Carl to go in with you?"

"I was afraid he might get hurt. I had a good idea that would go down ugly, and I didn't want Carl or Jane to get hurt. They never should have gone after a man like that."

"Can't argue with you there. It was the big score everybody looks for. They made enough this time to pay off their cabin up in Wisconsin.

Pretty place by a lake. They'll stick to the safe and easy stuff now and build up a retirement fund."

"Good to hear. So, what else has you walking on eggs?"

Morty sighed and looked at his desk. "I saw a new wanted poster at the police station yesterday."

"And?"

"It has your face on it. Says your name is Lenora Schmidt."

"Crap. Yeah, that used to be my name. I know what this is about. Looks like I have to go home to Bixby and tidy up a loose end. Did it say what I was wanted for?"

"Questioning."

"Okay, guess I'll be out of action for a week. See you later, Morty. Thanks for the coffee."

"Hey, Seeker. If you need bail money ..."

"Shut up, Morty." He was still chuckling as she walked out the door. Two days later she was back in Bixby.

Lenora walked into the police station and approached the desk. "Yes, Ma'am, can I help you?"

"My name is Lenora Schmidt. You guys put out a wanted poster on me. Why?"

"We did? Just a minute. Schmidt, Schmidt. Right, here we are. Officer Mundy has been trying to locate you. Just a minute now and I'll get him for you." He was soon back with an older officer who escorted her to his desk in the inner office.

"Now then, Miss Schmidt," he began, "just where have you been the past six months?"

"Here, there, and everywhere." He gave her a hard look. "It's my job."

"And what job would that be?"

"Bounty Hunter. I've been working under the name Lady Seeker."

"Seeker, Seeker, wait, you're that badass bounty hunter?" She just nodded. "You've brought in some pretty tough characters."

"They're not that tough."

"Oh?"

"After my father these guys are a bunch of wimps."

"Right, your father. That brings us to the point. Your father said you went crazy, beat your mother half to death then broke his arm and leg. What's your story about that day?"

"That was the day I left home for good. I gave him news he didn't want to hear. He hit me hard and I went down, bleeding. He turned on Mom then and I managed to crawl outside. I was bleeding a lot. I'll bet you guys found blood on the driveway."

"We did. If we test, will we match that to yours?"

"Oh yeah, it was mine all right. I lay there bleeding, listening to Momma screaming inside. When her screams stopped I knew I was finished if I didn't get up. I got to my feet and ran. He came after me. I made it to the river and slid down the bank. There's a lot of rocks and they're slippery. I made it down and across. He didn't. I heard him scream, turned back and he was laying there."

"Then what happened?"

"He asked me to help him and I said no. I climbed up the other side and ran. A girl in an old car picked me up. She wanted to take me to the hospital, but I wouldn't go. She used her first aid kit, patched me up, and eventually dropped me off in New York. I hit the streets, bummed around for a while, then decided I could make a living as a bounty hunter."

"All right. What do you think set your father off that day?"

"The only thing he ever loved was my younger sister, Belinda. She ran away from home, and I was sent to find her and bring her back. I found her in LA working in porn films. She refused to come with me. Father didn't take the news well."

The officer nodded. "Miss Schmidt, I have some bad news for you."

"Momma? Is she ...?"

"She's alive, but she'll never walk again. Your story jives pretty well with hers. She's gone to California to live with your sister."

"And Father?"

"In a prison hospital. He blew a temper tantrum and had a heart attack as a result. You can see him if you want."

"No thanks, I'm good this way."

"Okay, well, I guess that wraps it up. He's a big boy and his story about you breaking his leg sounded pretty farfetched."

"Officer Mundy, I was, and still am, deathly afraid of that man. I don't want to be anywhere near him ever again." She stood and started to leave, but his voice stopped her.

"There's just one thing that bothers me."

"Oh? What's that?"

"You said you're the Seeker, the bounty hunter. There was something about you and that vigilante, the Viper, in North Bay."

"That was a crazy day. I was working with two other people. Our guy was holed up in an old house in North Bay. Jane took the front door, Carl the back, and I got the unenviable task of going in after him. The place was full of men, booze, and guns."

"So what happened?"

"A line of BS got me close enough to the target to grab him. The others started grabbing guns, then the Viper appeared. I wasn't interesting anymore. When the dust settled Viper wanted to know what was up. I told him I need the target alive to get paid. He laughed at me and walked away.

"The Viper, now there's a real badass."

"So I've heard." Lenora was looking at him, waiting for another question. "All right, Miss Schmidt. I guess we're done here for now, unless you have something more to add."

"I don't, except to say I'll steer wide of North Bay from now on."

"That's smart. From what I hear this Viper would just walk through you and pay no attention at all. Okay, you can go."

"Thanks. Any chance you could pull that wanted poster of me? Doesn't look good to the boss, if you know what I mean."

He chuckled at that. "I'll pull it back right now."

She thanked him and walked out the door. Once back in the van with Roscoe, She got the shakes. "Lady Moragah?"

"I am here, my priestess."

"Moragah, I lied to that policeman. I lied up, down, and sideways. Am I doomed to hell?"

"Be at peace, my child. The place you speak of does not exist. Actually, I'm quite pleased with the way you managed to satisfy his curiosity, and yet remain free. It was well done."

"So, lying to the police isn't a mortal sin in your book?"

"As Kara would say, nope, just another weapon in the arsenal. Lenora, you did well here, have no fear. However, be wary, for I sense the police will be watching your adventures closely."

"Yeah, I get that same impression. I'll keep a sharp eye out. Ah well, it seems like we're done here. Might as well head for home."

"You wish to see your old home?"

"No, I meant back to Mary Jo's B&B. I want to see if Morty has any new cases for me." She started the van and drove away. A short while later she stopped at the same place where she and Penny had camped that first night.

Heather

Lenora took her time heading back. She was clear now, she could open a bank account and stop carrying so much cash in the van. The second night of her journey home she called Penny and brought her up to speed on her adventures. The next she stayed with Mary Jo.

Lenora awakened with the birds, took Roscoe for a long run then treated herself to a long shower. After a huge breakfast with Mary Jo she set out for town, first the bank, and then Morty's office. There was a woman there, chatting with Morty and Lenora sucked in her breath. She was startled by the woman's beauty and at her own reaction to it. "Oops, sorry folks. I'll come back later."

Morty's call stopped her at the door. "No, Seeker, wait. We were actually just talking about you and hoping you'd show up today."

"Really? Does this mean you've got another job for me?"

"Actually, I do." The brunette was stunning, and she favored Lenora with a smile that would melt polar ice. She'd noticed Lenora's reaction to her and decided to take advantage.

The woman had a sweet, yet low pitched voice. Lenora struggled to get her hormones under control. Dammit, a woman had never rocked her world like this before. Oh sure, she was a bit Bi, but this was different. She suspected Moragah changed something else in the priestess-making process. She turned away and poured herself a coffee.

Lenora sat and took a long sip of her coffee, and another long glance at the woman. "I'm listening."

"My name's Heather Jones. I'm a bail bonds-woman. I really need your help."

"They call me Lady Seeker, friends call me Lennie. Now, you need a bounty hunter, I get that, but why me in particular, and why come in person not knowing if I'd be here or not?"

"Lennie?"

"Short for Lenora."

"Pretty. I like it. All right, Lennie, I'll lay it out for you. This was my father's business. I inherited it a few months ago when my parents were killed."

"Wow. That's tough."

"Yes, it is. Worse, during the time between their deaths and my actually taking over, several people took advantage and left town. The truth is, I'm desperate here. I stand to lose everything unless I can recoup some of these losses."

"Thus the need for a bounty hunter. Why me?"

"I was whining to an old school chum and he recommended you. He said you're a better hunter than a dinner date."

Lenora nearly snorted her coffee, then chuckled. "Andy Blaise. He should talk. All through dinner he went on and on about his wife. So, Andy recommended me?"

"Seeker, he told me what you did. All of it, including the part where you disarmed him easily. He said you were working out of Hampton, so I phoned Uncle Morty. He listened to me, admitted he actually knows you, and agreed to help me."

"Oh? How?"

"I said I'd talk to you for Heather. Lennie, I knew her dad quite well. He was a business associate and a friend."

Lenora took another long sip from her coffee. "Okay, I get the need, and helping the daughter of an old friend, but why are the two of you putting the hard sell on me?"

"Hard sell?" asked Heather. "What do you mean, hard sell?"

"Oh come on. Morty is over there doing the puppy dog eyes thing, and you saw my reaction to you when I walked in. You've been pouring on the sexy ever since."

This time Heather laughed. It was a full rich laugh and Lenora was smitten all over again. "Busted. So, Lennie, is it working?"

"Too darn well. Come on, guys, what's the deal here?" Neither of them spoke, they just looked at each other. "Okay, it's been fun, folks. Nice meeting you, Heather."

She turned to go, but Heather's voice stopped her. "I'm broke, Seeker. Dead broke. I need to recoup some of those losses before I can clear the debts and pay you. Morty told me your creedo, you do the job and then you get paid, in cash. I can't do it. I need some time before I can pay."

Lenora turned back to face her. "How much time?"

"Two weeks after the first return?" Heather batted her eyelashes and looked hopeful.

"Tell me the truth, Morty. Is she good for it?"

"She's good for it, Seeker. If she doesn't pay within two weeks I'll make good on it."

Lenora didn't speak for a moment then sighed and resumed her chair. "This never leaves this room. As far as the rest of the world goes, I'm getting paid on delivery."

"Not a word, I swear it." Heather reached over to lightly grasp Lenora's arm, sending a thrill through her. "Seeker, thank you."

"Don't thank me yet, I still have to catch a few bad guys first. Got any paperwork with you?" For an answer Heather pulled a stack of file folders from her briefcase. She passed them over. "Sweet mother of mercy, how many are there?"

"That's the first five. There are eight more."

"That many ran out on you? Oh man, no wonder you're broke."

"It gets worse."

"Worse?"

"I have to make good on the top three there before I can work again."

"They pulled your ticket?" Heather just nodded. "Well crap. Guess it's time to get to work. Okay, who's closest?" She shuffled the files for a moment then pulled one out of the pile. "Jenine Baker, looks like you're up."

Lenora closed her eyes and began to turn in a circle, talking to the fugitive the whole time. "Come on, Jenine, tell me where you're hiding." Finally she stopped and opened her eyes. "Okay, I'm off. Where do I reach you?"

"Right here for the next little while," replied Heather.

"They locked down your office too?" She nodded. "Bummer. Okay, later folks." Lenora went outside and climbed into her van. They watched through the window as she drove away.

"There's just no understanding some people," muttered Lenora, as she drove towards the next town. "Now, if I'm lucky I can snag this one and deliver her the same day."

She got lucky. The woman was working in the kitchen of a run down cafe about three blocks from the police station. Lenora went in, called the woman's name, and a body blasted through the back door. Halfway down the alley Lenora had her. Ten minutes later she walked through the doors of the police station, holding her captive by the collar.

She was just getting her receipt and giving her statement when she heard a voice behind her. "Well, that didn't take you long." She turned to see Andy grinning at her.

Lenora smiled and patted his arm as she walked past on her way out the door. "Don't go away, folks. I'll be right back with more." She heard Andy's bellowing laugh as she walked back to the van. Lenore settled herself behind the wheel. "Okay, Roscoe, let's go get number two."

Six days later Lenora entered Morty's office again. She poured herself a coffee then fairly collapsed into a chair. She took a long pull from the mug then moaned with delight. "I've got to say, the coffee sure has improved around here since Heather moved in."

Morty looked up and grinned. "Can't argue that. How the hunting?"

"Better than average." Lenora pulled a fat envelope from her shoulder bag and tossed it to Heather. "There you go, pretty lady. You're on the hook for five captures. Toss me the other eight. I'll get started as soon as I finish my coffee."

"You got all five that fast? Jesus, Seeker. I don't want you to kill yourself. You need to get some rest."

"Ah, I'm tougher than I look."

"Listen, Super Seeker, you need to rest for a few days. What you've done here is a true miracle. This will get me back up and running. I swear I'll get your money to you the minute I have it."

"Easy, Heather. Get yourself re-established first. Once I head out again, you work on your debts and getting back in the game. We can settle up after things smooth out for you."

"Are you sure?"

"I'm sure. Get yourself right. then we'll settle up."

"Lennie, I can't thank you enough for all this. If there is ever anything I can do for you, just ask."

"Okay, will you go out with me?"

Heather's big blue eyes opened wide, then she saw the beginnings of a grin on Lenora's face. "Why sure, sugar. Where'll we go?"

"Across the street to that coffee shop. I can get something to eat there, and ..."

"Oh for pity sake. That's not food. Don't you have any food in that camper?"

"I've got some dog food, but Roscoe won't share."

"Dammit, Seeker, this won't do." Heather rose and grabbed her purse. "Give me your keys."

"My keys?"

"Yes, the keys to the camper. You're dead on your feet. You stretch out on the bunk while I get some groceries and make you a proper meal."

"Wow. Drop dead gorgeous and she cooks, too. How did I get so lucky?"

"If you think you're lucky now, just wait until you taste my cooking. Come on, Super Woman." She took Lenora by the hand and pulled her along. She unlocked the camper, fussed over Roscoe a bit then ordered them both onto the bunk at the back. Lenora was asleep by the time Heather parked the van at the supermarket.

Lenora was still sleeping when Heather returned. She smiled and put away the groceries then got into the driver's seat. When Lenora awakened the van was parked at a highway lookout point. It was dark outside, the sky was ablaze with stars, and Heather was in the driver's seat with it turned sideways. She was reading and Lenora smiled to see her. "Lady Moragah?"

"I am here, my daughter."

"Moragah, did you tweak my sexual preferences?"

"Yes, but in truth, you didn't need much tweaking. Are you upset?"

"Not a bit. I just wondered, that's all. Can I ask why?"

"The life of a priestess is often extremely dangerous. A child would be forever in danger, and few men can deal with a woman who is stronger, faster, and smarter who can be called to danger at any moment. In times past the priestesses kept each others hearts, as Kara and Tasha do now. However, Penny and Seline have found partners who can deal with the life they lead.

"I must say, Lenora. Heather is quite attractive. She is also very clever and far tougher than she appears to be. I believe you have chosen well."

"Yeah, well, that choice is hers to make. We need to take this slow and get to know each other a lot better first."

"Then I leave you to it." Lenora felt Moragah's mirth as She pulled back.

"Now there's a perfect sight to wake up to."

Heather smiled and turned to Lenora. "Well there you are, sleepyhead. Hungry?"

"Famished."

"All right. You take care of business while I get busy in the kitchen."

Lenora quickly tidied herself in the tiny toilet room, then took Roscoe out to get a leg in the air. He snuffled about for a bit, marked the best spot, then they returned to find a delicious dinner waiting for them. "Oh my god, Heather, this is pure magic," said Lenora as she devoured her meal. Smiling with delight, Heather dished up another portion for her. Lenora made short work of that one too.

"Wow, somebody was hungry." Heather took the empty plate and put it in the tiny sink.

"Was, but no longer. Heather, that was awesome. Not only gorgeous, but she cooks, too. I think I'm in love, Roscoe."

"Joke all you want, Lady Seeker, but you have to take better care of yourself."

"Yeah, well, I usually do, but I thought we were on the clock with this one."

"We are, yes, but not at the expense of your health. Jesus woman, what you've done is a miracle, but I don't want you killing yourself, not for me."

"No? You want me alive?"

Heather laughed and Lenora thought she'd do anything to make her laugh like that. "Yes, you shameless flirt, I do want you alive. Now, stop flirting and be serious."

"Heather?"

"You got my sad story. Now I want yours. How did a sweet country girl like you end up as a bounty hunter anyway?"

Lenora slid over onto the bunk then leaned back. "That's quite a story. You sure you want to hear it?"

Heather joined her on the bunk, sitting cross legged and facing her. "Come on, Lennie. Tell me a story."

"Okay, but first, two things. I don't want any sympathy, and I really don't want you to call the guys in white coats with the butterfly nets."

Heather wrinkled her brow and gazed into Lenora's eyes. "Okay, no sympathy and no straight jackets. Look, Lennie, if you don't want ..."

"Actually, Heather, I do want. I want you to know about me for several reasons."

"Okay, girl. I'm listening."

"Where do I start, at the beginning, I guess. I know you had a loving family, and it hurts that you lost that so soon. I didn't, and a piece of me is a tiny bit jealous. My father is a violent and brutal man. He physically and emotionally abused my mother, and me as well, as long as I can remember.

"On the day my life changed forever, I was lying on the driveway, dying. Face broken, ribs punched through lungs, broken bones in my eyes and nose, loose teeth, and more. I was bleeding out internally as well as externally."

"Lenora, Jesus ..."

Lenora patted her hand and went on. "I was fading, and listening to my mother scream, when I heard a voice in my mind. At the sound of that voice all my pain went away. It was the voice of Moragah."

"Moragah?"

"Moragah, Goddess of Wisdom, Defender of the Weak."

"Never heard of that one."

"She's real, Heather. She offered to heal my wounds if I would listen to what she had in mind. That was an easy one. I went for it. I felt the injuries healing, bones knitting back together, teeth moving back into place, lungs clearing, and I felt stronger than ever before in my life. I jumped to my feet and ran.

"A short while later I took refuge under a highway bridge. I listened to Moragah as she showed me her other priestesses, Lady Blue, Little

Blue, Lady Justice, and Lady Shadow." Lenora stopped. She gazed at Heather then sighed and went on. "Okay, I can see you think these people are just urban legends, and that I'm crazy as a loon. Please, just hear me out.

"Moragah said she needed a Seeker. She wouldn't say why or when, just that she might need one. If I would agree to become that Seeker she would grant me super powers. At that point I could hear my father coming for me. I took the deal. That's when I changed, when She changed me.

"Heather, I can do what I do because I'm faster and stronger than any ten men. I can climb sheer walls, hear at great distance, and I can find anyone or anything if I want to. All I have to do is want to know where they are. Girl, you saw me do it the day we met." Heather wasn't speaking. Her eyes were huge and her mind was racing.

"Heather, take my hands."

"What?"

"I won't hurt you, girl. Just take my hands."

Reluctantly, Heather reached out and placed her hands in Lenora's. Instantly she felt the vast presence of Moragah engulf them. *Do not fear so, my child. Lenora has spoken the truth, but she has softened the true scope of her injuries and the abilities I have given her."*

"You're real. A real goddess. Until this moment I didn't believe gods, any gods, were real."

"Speaking for myself," chuckled Moragah, *"I believe I am quite real. Heather, I see the ache in your heart for the loss of your parents. Be at peace, my child. Death is not the end of the spirit's journey, merely a passage to another step on the path. Heather, Lenora will help you all she can, but you must keep her secrets. Her life would soon become a hell if the public learned of her abilities. She, too, must become the stuff of urban legends. Will you keep the faith with us?"*

"I will, I promise. Thank you for revealing yourself to me, but I have to wonder why."

"Do you not know, Heather? Can you not see Lenora's feelings for you? It is for her that I reveal myself to you. To show her you are worthy of her trust. Don't be afraid. I won't interfere, nor will I try to influence you in any way. The relationship between you is for you two to create or not as you choose. Be well, my child." With that Moragah withdrew.

"Well, shit, that was seriously wild. This is the first time a date introduced me to a real goddess. How do you plan to top that one?"

Lenora laughed with delight. "Oh lord, the pressure. Heather, that's how I became a bounty hunter. What else would I do, given a skill set like that?"

"As wild as it is, that does explain how you do it, how you find them, and how you bring them down even though they're armed and in a group. Lennie, you can still be hurt though, right? If you got shot ...?"

"Oh yeah, I can be hurt, killed. I'm careful, Heather. Really careful."

"You'd better be. Now, about this relationship thing."

"Easy woman, don't shoot. I can't help it you have me bedazzled. I ..."

"Will give me time, that's what you'll do. Please? I'm not averse to the idea, and I'll admit I'm intrigued by you, but I've never dated a girl before."

"Me neither. No idea at all how it's supposed to work."

"Slow, it's supposed to work slow."

"Okay, but it is at work, right? A work in progress?"

"Can we just go easy and see how it evolves?"

"All right, Heather, you're the boss. We'll let it evolve. We can start as soon as I get back."

"Get back? Where are you going?"

"Hunting, girl. I've got eight more to bring in, right?"

"Please be careful, Lennie. I know you have super powers, but be careful anyway. For me?"

Lenora grinned. "Girl, I'd do anything for you."

"Oh yeah, I am so going to abuse that one. Now, take me home, it's getting late."

Lenora drove back to Morty's offices and watched until she was safely away in her car. When Heather returned the next morning she found a note taped to the door. "Heather, thanks for yesterday. Gone hunting. See you when I get back. Lennie."

Not Always Cut and Dried

Lenora sat quietly beneath a bridge, Roscoe beside her and a man, bound hand and foot, lying nearby. She was tired and thinking of Heather. She could hear the man quietly rubbing his bound hands against a jagged rock, trying to cut through the knots. "Franklin, you ruin that rope I'll break your hands and claim you did it to yourself."

He froze, then sighed. "This is all wrong, I'm innocent."

"Really? You didn't kill those three men? You didn't jump bail after the bond for a million dollars was posted?"

"All right, yes, I killed those men. They kidnapped my daughter and raped her. They had it coming."

"Can't argue that."

"So let me go."

"Nope. Can't do it."

"Look, this is wrong, and you know it. They're asking for the death penalty, for Christ's sake."

"Shut up, Franklin. Just shut the hell up, I don't want to hear it."

"Hear what? That an innocent man is getting persecuted? A twelve-year-old was raped and her father is being railroaded for killing the men who did it? That the system is corrupt? That I rescued my child and now she's in foster care because I defended her? That ..."

"I said shut up. Dammit, I'll gag you and tie you on the roof of the camper if I have to. For fuck's sake, what's a girl have to do to get a bit of peace and quiet around here?"

He lay still for a moment. "This is all screwed up and it's wrong. You know I'm right."

"I'm not arguing that, but that's not the point, not for me."

"What is the point for you, Bounty Hunter? The money? The need and greed for money has poisoned the entire goddamned country. I should have known you'd be like all the rest."

"It's not about the money, Franklin, at least not the way you think."

"No, so what's it about then? What's it all for? What's it really about for you?"

"You jumped bail, I find you, I bring you back to face trial, and I get paid. Roscoe gets his favorite brand of dog food, and I get gas for the van. We live free another day. That's another day the banks don't own me, the big money guys can't jerk a job out from under me and destroy me. We run free another day, and we stay on the right side of the law to do it."

"How very fucking noble and comfortable for you. You get the life you want and to hell with everybody else."

"I'll tell you a story, Franklin. Once upon a time there was a pretty girl studying to be a veterinarian. A drunk driver killed her parents and she was jerked out of school to take over her father's business. She was new, inexperienced, and in mourning. She posted bail for a bunch of assholes who ran out on her. She lost the business, her home, and everything her father had spent a lifetime building. She's also on the hook for the goddamned student loans.

"The bright spot in this story is, she can get some of it back if I can retrieve the assholes that broke her. You, my friend, are a star member of that club. So here's what happens. I take you back, the nice lady is off the hook, gets a piece of her life back, and I get paid. I'm not going any deeper into this shit than that. Between you and me, I think you did the right thing. Under the same circumstances I'd do the same. Now shut the hell up and let me think."

"So there's no real justice in the world for you either, is there?"

"Nope, not a damn bit of it, but I do know where to find it. What's your daughter's name?"

"What?"

"Your daughter, what's her name?"

"Why do you want to know?"

"So I can find her and let her know you're all right."

"Sally. Sally Jean Franklin. I have no idea where they put her though. She's in the system somewhere."

"The name is all I need." Lenora stood up and started to walk away.

"Hey, where are you going?"

"To bed. I'm tired and need some rest."

"You're just going to leave me here? Jesus woman, you can't just leave me here in the open all tied up."

"The hell I can't. And you'd damn well better be there when I come back for you in the morning. I found you easy, took you down easy, but if I have to chase you again all bets are off. Savvy?"

He sighed deeply and accepted his defeat. "I won't run. Bounty Hunter, about Sally. Thanks for that."

"Sure." Lenora climbed back up to her van then called Roscoe in and gave him a biscuit. She sank heavily onto the bed and sighed. "Roscoe, old buddy, I'm about to cross the line here. I hope you still respect me in the morning." He just wagged his tail and settled down with his head in her lap.

Lenora closed her eyes and began to concentrate. She found Lady Justice easily enough. Swallowing her initial fear of the woman, she began to concentrate harder. Slowly the woman with the cold eyes turned to her. After a moment of searching, she smiled, and the smile reached her eyes. She changed from a cold warrior to a pretty young woman.

Robert Franklin lay beneath that old bridge trying to sleep. She'd taken him easily, as she'd said. Running from her would be useless, and he knew it. He'd squirmed around, trying to get comfortable, but it didn't help much. It was going to be a long night. And then he heard her coming back.

She slipped the ropes off his feet and easily stood him up. "It's warmer and more comfortable in the van. Come on."

She took him up and tied him in the passengers seat, tilting it back so he could sleep. The next morning she made him breakfast then turned him in at the police station. Just before they entered the building she spoke softly. "Stay alert, and pay attention over the next few days." He was puzzled by that, but she said nothing more.

Six days later, as he sat in his cell mulling over his fate, he heard a soft noise outside. Puzzled, he sat up straighter and listened. There was a voice. "Franklin?"

"Here."

"Be ready." Suddenly the lights went out and the bars across the window were ripped away. "Come!" A hand was extended through the window as the emergency power came on. He was practically hauled through the opening and slung across powerful shoulders. They were three stories up. He clung tightly to his savior as he was carried swiftly down the sheer wall. There was no climbing gear he could see.

A car was waiting with the motor running. He was shoved inside, and his rescuer leaped behind the wheel. The car sped away. In the back seat Robert Franklin had tears in his eyes as he hugged his daughter fiercely. The masked driver eventually pulled over and got out. It was a woman.

"Franklin, the tank's full, it'll get you to Georgia City. There's a place marked on the map in the glove box. Go there, ask for sanctuary."

"Sanctuary?"

"That area is controlled by a bunch of war veterans. They're heavily armed and the police won't go into their territory. I asked someone to meet you there. Her name is Justice, tell her your story. This car is stolen so don't waste any time, just drive. Oh, and never tell a living soul what happened here tonight except Lady Justice."

"I won't, I swear."

She walked away towards the shadows. He got behind the wheel and drove swiftly away. "I owe you one, Bounty Hunter," he whispered as he headed for the highway north.

Lenora sighed as she pulled off the mask. She sank into the driver's seat, but didn't start the van. "Lady Moragah, please tell me you're not mad at me for doing this."

"On the contrary, my priestess. I'm quite pleased with you, and proud of the way you managed it. The child is reunited with her father, Tasha will see them safe with her people, and you waited long enough for Heather to be clear of any costs attached to his disappearance. Lenora, you managed to help Heather who was powerless to help herself, and yet you defended the weak by reuniting the family and finding them Sanctuary. Go to bed now, my daughter. I will guard your rest this night."

With a sigh of relief Lenora went back and crawled into the bunk. Roscoe hopped up beside her and settled down. Outside a dense patch of fog formed in the area, and nothing at all went near the old van.

"That's the last of them, folks and family." Lenora tossed the thick folder on the desk and accepted the coffee Heather passed to her. She settled back into a chair, grinning.

Morty just shook his head. "Well, you look pretty pleased with yourself."

"I am, Morty, I am. I got 'em all. All eight of them. It's done, right, pretty lady? That's all of them?"

"That's all of them, Lennie. My god, you're pure magic. I can't believe what you've managed to do in so short a time. So, when was the last time you had a decent meal?"

"When was the last time you cooked for me?"

"Lenora, for god's sake. You've got to take better care of yourself. Geez woman. I'll bet there's nothing but dog food in that van either."

Lenora sighed. "Busted. Might be a can of beans, but ..." She took another long sip of the coffee and moaned with delight.

"Woman, what am I going to do with you?"

"Have dinner with me tonight?"

Heather grinned. "Dinner, huh? Am I cooking?"

"You'll have to. I'm flat broke."

"I can fix that," said Morty. He placed a briefcase on his desk and popped it open. It was filled with stacks of bills. "It's all there, Seeker. Every dollar Heather owes."

"Wow. That's awesome, but you don't have to go crazy on me, guys. Heather, I said to take your time and get back on your feet before ..."

Heather stepped over, bent and kissed Lenora on the cheek. "Lady Seeker does the job, and then she gets paid. Those are the rules. You're buying dinner tonight."

"Count on it. Heather, look me in the eye, both of you look me in the eye. Tell me this isn't going to cause problems for you, either of you. I don't want to break anybody's back here."

"It won't, Lennie," replied Heather. "We had a business arrangement and now that contract has been met. Now we're clear of that."

"That was never an issue for me, pretty lady."

"I know, but it was for me. Now we're on an even keel we can proceed with that other thing."

"Other thing?"

"You know, the relationship thing."

Lenora grinned. "Oh, right. That thing. Okay, what's the next step?"

"You buy me dinner."

"Love to." Lenora was smiling and so was Heather.

"Seeker, you heard the news?" asked Morty.

"What news?"

"Apparently, one of those jokers you brought in last week broke jail."

"Oh?"

"Yeah, he must have had help outside. Somebody cut the power to the jailhouse and blew out the window of his cell. Got away clean. His kid disappeared from the foster home too. They're on the run now. Could be anywhere."

"Wow. Tell me you're not on the hook for that, are you, Heather?"

"No, you brought him in and everything was processed properly. The cops lost him so he's the state's problem now."

"Well that's good to know. At least I don't have to run him down again. Everything worked out for the best then."

"Seems so." Heather, gave Lenora a penetrating look. "Anyway, we have more news." Lenora was grateful for the change of subject. "Uncle Morty bought out my business then took me on as a full partner."

"Really?"

"Yes," said Morty. "Heather will be working out of this office permanently. One of us will have to commute to the branch office two or three times a week, but we'll take turns at that."

"Well now, I guess I'll have to hang around the office a lot more."

"Sure," grinned Morty, "but with that big payday, you're buying the coffee."

"Works for me. I'll just go drop this in the bank then catch a nap before our big date tonight."

"The bank?"

"Yeah, the bank. I know, Morty, I know. The world's gone all to hell. Lady Seeker actually got a bank account. Pick you up here at five, Heather?"

"I'll be waiting." They were both smiling at her as she left the office.

Five o'clock arrived and so did Lenora, driving a car and wearing a dress. Heather didn't recognize her at first. When she realized who it was she broke into a bright smile. "Oh my god. Lennie. Girl, you clean up right nice, you do. A dress too?"

Lenora laughed and blushed at the same time. "Yeah, I had to go shopping 'cause I didn't own one. When I left home I left with the clothes on my back. Truth is, I like to girl up a bit, but life has been all about boots and jeans lately." She smiled as she installed Heather in the old car then got behind the wheel.

"A car, too?"

"All right, Miss Curiosity, I'll talk. A friend gave me this old car shortly after I left home. When I got some money ahead I bought the van from the sweetest lady. Then I rented the garage from her to store the car in. She's opened a small B&B just outside town. Her name's Mary Jo and she uses the car when I'm away, which is most of the time, but tonight I left Roscoe with her and brought the car."

Heather nodded. "Sorry to be such a nosy bug, but I can't help it. Usually I have no problem minding my own business, but I can't seem to where you're concerned."

"Oh? Now why is that?"

"Can't say. I guess it's because I want to know all about you. Please don't be offended."

"I'm not. Thrilled is more like it. What else do you want to know?"

"About the dress. You look comfortable, relaxed, happy. Completely at ease."

"I spent most of my formative years in skirts. Father didn't approve of women wearing pants. You're right, I actually feel more at ease in skirts. Now, that's a national secret. That information is need to know only, pretty lady."

Heather's laugh brought a bright smile to Lenora's face.

They chatted easily over dinner, then Lenora drove up to the lookout where Heather had parked the van days before. The night was warm, and cloudy, no stars to see, but the city lights were beautiful. Lenora reached for Heather's hand and delicate fingers laced together with her own.

"Okay, now I'm the curious one. What's the real deal with you and Morty teaming up?"

"Uncle Morty was Dad's best friend. He bought up the business because I couldn't get anywhere with it. After the mess I made of it, no one would trust me. He bought me out and will teach me the ropes. Once I get some experience under my belt he'll start easing back a bit. He's alone in the world too, Lennie. He has no one to pass the torch to, if you know what I mean."

"Yeah, I get it. Makes a lot of sense. I ... what is it, Heather? What's wrong?"

Heather had stopped walking and was staring at the sky. "Oh god, that can't be real." She was visibly frightened. "Behind you, in the sky. It looks like a ..."

"Dragon. Shit, there goes the evening. Stay close to me; it'll be okay, I promise."

"Lennie?"

"Just stay close." Heather stepped in behind Lenora and clung to her arm.

By this time, the beast was near enough for the sound of mighty wings to reach them. Suddenly it folded those wings and plummeted towards the ground. The wings snapped open at the last second with a sound like thunder. It was huge, fire dancing from its nostrils as it alit easily a short distance from them. There was a rider on its back.

With startling speed and a liquid grace the creature dismounted and strode toward them. It was a woman, but not human. She moved like a warrior. Reaching them she swept back the hood of her cloak to reveal emerald green eyes, flame red hair braided and tossed carelessly across one shoulder, and up swept ears. When she spoke her voice was deep, rich, and commanding. "Seeker, I require a moment of your time."

Lenora tucked Heather a bit more behind her. "Of course. How can I be of service, Lady Shadow?"

The elf waved a hand and a man appeared. Heather could see through him, obviously an illusion, a hologram. "I seek this man. He has reached this city, but I cannot locate him. Time is of the essence."

"Give me his name."

"Leonard Brill."

Lenora nodded then closed her eyes. "Talk to me, Leonard. Where are you. Talk to me... ah, there you are. All right now, pulling it back a bit, street sign, I need a ...yes. Peach Tree Avenue. Numbers now, okay there's the building. Number 13746 Peach Tree Ave. Apartment 407. He's there watching TV. He's alone, but armed, keeping a close eye on the door."

The hologram man vanished. "Excellent. Live well, Seeker. Run free."

"Hunt well, Lady Shadow."

Lenora was already talking to the woman's back. The elf warrior leaped aboard the dragon's back, and with a scream of challenge and a thunderous beat of vast leathery wings, it leaped into the sky. A moment later it vanished into the clouds.

Heather's knees were shaking and she was clinging to Lenora. "Lennie, hold me up please. My legs don't want to work."

Lenora turned slightly to take Heather in her arms. She held her gently and cooed soothing sounds until the girl stopped shaking. "Sweet baby Jesus, Lennie, what the hell was that?"

"Sorry, pretty lady. I was just trying to top the excitement of the first date."

"What? What are you ... oh you beast, you're teasing me. I can't believe you're teasing me when I'm here scared to death and begging you for protection. You're awful."

"I know. I'm a bad woman."

"Yes you are, a thoroughly bad woman. Lennie, did that really happen? Was that real?"

"Yes, pretty lady, it was real. That, my dear Heather, was Lady Shadow in the flesh. I think the dragon's name is Aeroth."

"What? Stop it, Lenora. I don't give a rat's ass what the dragon's name is. You have to stop this."

"Stop what?"

"Grinning at me for starters. Making legends and fantasy come true for another."

"Sorry."

"Lady Shadow is real?"

"Yup. Maybe next time I'll get to introduce you. And before you ask, no, I didn't set this up. The last thing I want to do is scare you away."

Heather was beginning to get her good humor back. "Oh yeah? So, what do you want to do with me?"

Lenora laughed with delight. "Pretty lady, if I tell you that you'll beat me up. However, I'll confess, holding you like this is nice."

Heather laid her head on Lenora's shoulder. "Yes it is. I feel safe with you. I know some of what you can do, but I still feel safe with you."

"You're shaking. I think you've just had a big adrenaline dump, and now you're getting the shakes from that. Pretty lady, I'm taking you for a hamburger. Ah, ah, no arguments. You need to power up again. I'm sorry Shadow frightened you."

"She doesn't scare you, does she?"

"Oh yes, she does. I have super powers compared to you. Shadow has super powers compared to me. I've met her in human form and she's a sweetie, fun to hang out with. Shadow is her warrior self. Not to be messed with. Come on now, we're going for that burger."

"Lennie, about this dating thing, I don't think I can take any more of this."

Lenora's world shattered. Reluctantly, she let her arms fall away from Heather. "Okay, pretty lady, I understand."

"No, you don't. I'm telling you the dating thing will be the death of me. Can we just move past that part and go directly into the relationship thing?"

"Heather?"

"Lennie, I picked your brain for your life story, stuck my nose into your business, and you've been nothing but gentle and respectful with me. However, if you keep upping the ante every date I'll die of a heart attack before we ever get to the good part."

"All right, I was never allowed to date or have relationships when I was a kid, so I have no idea what to do next. You'll have to lead the way on this one. What's the next step?"

"First you kiss me like you mean it, then you feed me that burger, and then take me home and kiss me good night."

"Works for me." Lenora smiled as she gently tightened her arms around Heather again, and then kissed her softly. Heather was trembling and Lenora fought herself to keep from taking advantage. She thoroughly enjoyed the kiss, then tucked Heather back into the car.

Lenora walked her to the door and Heather unlocked it. "You're going back to the office?"

"There's a room upstairs where I'm camping until I find an apartment I can afford. Come in for a minute."

"Okay. What's up, pretty lady?"

"You are, we are."

"Uh-oh." Lenora closed the door and allowed Heather to lead her to the back, then up the stairs. She hadn't spoken, just waiting for Heather. Once inside the tiny old apartment, Heather turned and stepped into Lenora's arms again. This time the kiss had some fire in it and Lenora's knees were shaking. She moaned with delight and desire as their lips slowly parted.

"We need to talk."

"What? Now? First you fog up my brain so I can't think, and then you want to talk? Pretty lady, just what are you up to?"

"I'm sorry, Lennie, I am. I'm just trying to figure out where I fit in. What my role, my place, is in your life. You've got super powers, you earn more than I ever will, and you've got a goddess and a dragon rider for friends and ..."

"And I've been completely besotted since the first moment I saw you, pretty lady."

"You keep calling me that. Is that all I am to you? Eye candy?"

"Hardly." Lenora smiled and lightly kissed the tip of Heather's nose. "Heather, I call you that because that's one, but only one, of the things about you that amazes me. I've never seen anyone so physically perfect. However, there's more, so much more."

"Tell me, please. I need to hear it."

"You take charge, organize me, bully me into taking better care of myself, you show genuine concern for me. I've never truly encountered that before except from Penny."

"Who's Penny?"

"Lady Blue. I'll introduce you one day."

"Is she as scary as Shadow?"

"Oh hell no, nobody is scary as Shadow. Trust me. Pretty lady, you fill a deep hole in my world. I feel complete with you near me and only when you're near me. I've tried not to push ..."

"And you haven't, Lennie. At every step you've given me time to find my way, to evaluate my feelings ..."

"So, what happened tonight, aside from Shadow messing up our date, I mean."

"That's it in a nutshell. She did mess up our date. When my world suddenly went all to hell, and grew a lot bigger than I imagined it could be, you protected me. You knew we were safe, but you also knew I didn't know that. You put me behind you and protected me. At no point did I consider running away, jumping in the car to escape, or anything but holding on to you."

"Thanks for that. I'd have panicked if you'd run."

"Lennie, you made me feel safe, valued, and more. The purpose of dating is to discover if you enjoy each other's company. To learn if you feel safe with your partner or not. Okay, I'm past that part and ready for the next step, but I need to know I can be of value to you, not just now for my looks, but in the future when my looks fade."

"So that's it. Pretty lady, your smile lights up my world and you're certainly easy on the eye. However, if that's all it was I never would have asked you out, I'd just have hung around the office and drooled over you. So, here's some of the rest.

"Life threw you a major curve then beat you down when you couldn't handle it all by yourself. It beat you down, but it didn't break you. You gathered what resources you had left and went looking for a solution to the problem. With no super powers, and no real allies, you still didn't quit, you fought your way through. Pretty lady, I love your strength, courage, your tenacity, your intelligence, and especially the way you nurture me. I can honestly say, I never want to have a day without you in it."

Heather leaned her head on Lenora's shoulder. "Lennie, stay with me tonight?"

"Did I hear that right?"

"Yes, you incurable tease, you heard right."

"Wow, I'm going to wear a dress more often."

Heather laughed at that. "Stop it, you nut. Stop it and kiss me like you mean it." Lenora was more than happy to oblige.

Back on the Hunt

Morty entered the office to find Heather brewing coffee. "Something odd is going on. Jimmy says that old car has been parked outside all night. So, do you know anything about ...?"

"That's my car, Morty." Lenora gave him a bright smile and headed for the coffee pot while Heather blushed deeply.

"A dress, Seeker? You spent the night?"

"Yes, a dress. I am a girl after all, and yes, I spent the night. You have no real security on this old place, and I didn't want Heather to be alone and unprotected."

"Really? That's your story?"

"Yup, and I'm sticking to it."

"Gods, both of you are evil." Heather sighed then faced her mentor. "Uncle Morty ..."

"Easy girl, I have no problems here. None at all. Actually, Lennie's right. I do need better protection on this place. Especially if you're staying here."

"Yeah, about that, ..."

Morty shook his head. "Oh no. Oh no you don't, either one of you. Think this through. Come on Seeker, you know you can't take her with you on the hunt."

"Wasn't planning to, Morty. What we do want to do is get an apartment. I need a home base and Heather needs a home."

"Heather?"

"It's okay, Uncle Morty. Lennie's right. I know I'm not ready to go hunting with her, but I can look after the business end of it for her and make a home for her to come back to."

Lenora sighed and sank into a chair. "I was right, wasn't I? You used every cent you got for your business to pay me off."

"Yes, I did. Lennie, I wanted the relationship with you too, but not if I was owing you. That would never work, and you know it."

Suddenly the voice of Moragah sounded in Lenora's mind. *"Lenora, this is a good man and he can be trusted, both of them can. You must tell him, or he will never stop poking into your business, your past, trying to protect Heather."*

"I know, Lady Moragah. Okay, stand by. It's show and tell time.

"Morty, I can tell by the look on your face you think Heather might be using me, taking advantage without meaning to. I'll tell you truly, it ain't so. Heather knows a lot about me that no one else in the world knows. Now I'm going to tell you, so you'll understand."

She told him all of it. She even introduced him to Moragah. In the end he just sat in his chair, trying to absorb it all. "So you're really a super hero?"

"I'm no hero, Morty, just a gal with a special skill set. As you can see, I need Heather to keep me grounded. I also need to protect her."

"And you need some closet space."

Morty looked puzzled again. "Closet space?"

Heather nodded. "Somebody had to go buy a dress before she took me out. I mean, she lives in a camper for pity's sake."

The look on his face told them he didn't understand. "I'm two people, Morty. Up until now you've only met Lady Seeker." Lenora stood up and did a full turn. "This is the real Lenora."

"Not bad," came a soft male voice from the doorway. They turned to see a native man standing there, boots, jeans, buckskin jacket, and long braids. There was mirth in those dark eyes and a slight grin playing at his lips. "For a white girl."

"Okay, I'll take that as a compliment. How can we help you?"

"I'm looking for the Seeker."

"You found me."

"You're the one who kicked Andy Blaise's ass?"

"Yup. Want a demonstration?"

"I'm good."

His grin was getting wider, and Lenora found herself liking this guy. She matched his grin. "Okay, handsome, what can I do for you?"

"I've been tracking a man for three years. I need your help to pin him down."

"Three years? That's a long time to stay on a man's trail."

"He's my brother. He's good. Every time I get close he disappears."

"So, how do you know Andy?"

"We were in the academy together. I put in a few years on the force, but ..."

"Not your thing?"

"Long story. Look, Seeker, Andy says you have rules and don't come cheap. He also said you sometimes help people just because you can."

"Oh?"

"I can do about half that. I've got five thousand, that's all I could raise."

"You drink coffee?"

"Sure."

Heather suddenly came to life. "Here, I'll get it for you. Come in, sit. Cream and sugar?"

"Black."

"Purist."

Lenora grinned at him and he laughed. "Got used to it when I was broke too long."

She accepted a refreshed mug from Heather's hand then sat beside him, crossing her long legs. "Talk to me, handsome. Tell me a story."

He smiled shyly, took a sip of the coffee then began. "I'm Jack Longtree. My brother is Jimmy Longtree. He's a couple of years older than me. He left the reservation looking for work about ten years ago. Took me a while, but I finally got him to admit he'd joined the military. He did a tour oversea while paying for my college and training.

"Three years ago I was approached by the FBI. Jimmy had been mustered out and disappeared into the streets. He got mixed up with some bad people doing bad things."

"Drugs?"

"Yeah, and lots of them, Seeker. The DEA busted up the people he was working for, but a few of them got killed in the sting. Jimmy got away. I was on the force with Andy at the time. I was ordered to help them bring my brother in."

"So you quit the force?"

"I did, yeah. No way I was turning on my brother. The trouble is, now they follow me everywhere and Jimmy can smell them a mile away."

"So he eludes you to stay out of their clutches."

"Pretty much."

"Why are they so hell bent on bringing him in if they've already busted up the people he was working for?"

"I think it might be personal. The agent in charge of the file has a scar down his right cheek. Word has it, Jimmy gave him that."

Lenora nodded. "Okay. Just what is it you want me to do, Jack?"

"Get me close enough to him to talk to him. I need to know if he's all right, where his head is at. I won't ask you to cross the feds, just to help me get around them."

Lenora sat back, thinking. He didn't disturb her. Finally she sighed and looked to Heather. "Can you do it, honey?"

That *honey* gave Lenora a thrill and she beamed a bright smile at her lover. "I think so, pretty lady. Jack, it'll help a lot if you know the agent's name."

"I do. Got a picture of him too if that'll help."

"It will, but not right now. First for Jimmy Longtree." She stood and stepped away from him to an open space in the room. Closing her eyes, she began to call softly to Jimmy. It took only a moment then she stopped and nodded. "Okay, he's your brother all right. Easy to see the resemblance. He's about two days from here. Now for the fed."

"He's across the street, Seeker," said Morty. "Plain brown car, man behind the wheel reading a newspaper. Man's old school. That won't hide you anymore. He should be reading from his phone."

Lenora nodded. "Heather?"

"I believe this man, sweetheart. Can you help him?"

"I can, but only if you say so."

"Promise you'll be extra careful."

"I swear it, and I'll call every day."

"You'd better."

Lenora grinned. "Okay, Jack, go out the back and disappear. Here's an address. Go there and ask for a room for the night, tell Mary Jo I sent you. I'll pick you up later and we'll get on the hunt."

"What about the fed?"

"Leave him to me. Morty, Heather, when that fed comes asking questions, tell him the truth. Jack came in, hired the bounty hunter then they left together through the back door. Sweetie, could you get the car back to Mary Jo for me?"

"Sure, when?"

"Later this afternoon?"

"Done deal." Suddenly Heather stepped into Lenora's arms and kissed her deeply. "That's so you don't forget me."

"I could never forget you, my pretty lady. Find us a home. Roscoe and I'll be back before you know it." Another quick kiss and she was out the door with Jack.

She put Jack in a cab to Mary Jo's B&B then headed to the bank. She picked up a bundle of cash then returned to the office and gave it to

Heather. A hug, another kiss, then she was gone. She, too, took a cab to Mary Jo's. By dusk they were well out on the highway west. It was long past dark when she stopped.

"Not much of a talker, are you, Jack?"

"Not a lot to say, Seeker. You sure you know what you're doing?"

"I do. There's a pull out. Roscoe needs to get a leg in the air, and I need to stretch." She pulled over and they got out. Roscoe did his business then bullied Jack into a game of tug o' war.

Lenora smiled at them. "Looks like you get along better with animals than people."

He grinned as he let Roscoe win. "Pretty much."

"So, why'd you really leave the police force, Jack?"

"I told you. I won't hunt my brother, not for them. The force is totally corrupt, but you knew that already."

"Yeah, pretty much. There's a lot of good cops out there, Jack."

"Plenty of bad ones too. The thing is, there's no justice anywhere, not for my people."

"Not much for any people. Yeah, I know, easy words coming from a white girl. That doesn't hold the same charm it used to. Now you have to be white and rich or you're just dirt on the floor."

"That why your fee is so high?"

"Part of it, but mostly it's just to keep gas in the tank and dog food in the cupboard. You see, when I started this I had no idea there was so much money to be made. None. I was just hoping to stay off the streets."

"Then you met your spirit partner, your twin self. The one you called the pretty lady."

"Yup, that's about it."

"I envy you that."

"Never happen for you?"

"Oh yeah, it did. Car accident two years ago. She didn't make it."

"Harsh."

"Yeah, it is. Go call your woman now, let her know you're okay."

"Yes, boss."

Lenora rose and pulled her phone from the back pocket of her jeans. She returned a while later, grinning. Jack gave her a questioning look. "It seems the feds are pissed."

"Oh?"

"Yeah. They're having a bit of car trouble." He didn't speak, just gave her a questioning look. She winked at him then lifted the front of the van high in the air. That opened his eyes wide. She set it down gently then brushed her hands off on her jeans. "Apparently, while they were having lunch, some vandals managed to flip their car onto its roof."

He just shook his head and grinned. "What are you, Seeker?"

"I'm a priestess of Moragah, Goddess of Wisdom and Defender of the Weak."

"Right, and you have super strength."

"Yup, among other things. I ... shit, Jimmy's on the move. He's coming right at us and he's in a hurry. Still a long way off though." She turned back and paused for a moment. "The feds are still in town. Looks like we're good here for now."

"What do you mean?"

"We've lost the feds and Jimmy is headed this way in a hurry. It's late, might as well wait for him, right?"

"If you say so. Got a plan to get him to stop and say hello?"

"Working on that part. I get the bunk, you get the passenger's seat."

He grinned and shook his head. "I'm good out here. Got a blanket?" Lenora nodded then climbed into the van and tossed him the spare blanket.

She awakened in the morning to find him sitting beside a small fire. He watched silently as she faced the rising sun and thanked Moragah for her night's rest. "So, you're an outdoorsy guy, Mr. Traditional Camper?"

"Nah, I used a Zippo to start the fire." He smiled with delight as she laughed.

"Just be a minute." She closed her eyes for a moment then sighed. "Okay, the feds are on their way, but a long way off yet. Jimmy is almost here. We've got time for breakfast. Roscoe, what'd ya say, hot dogs for breakfast?" His answer was an enthusiastic bark. She brought out two packs and the long forks.

Jack thanked her and stuck a hotdog on a fork. As he turned it near the fire he spoke. "Did you work on that plan to slow Jimmy down?"

"Yeah, there's a couple of options."

"Such as?"

"I could put that dress back on and do the helpless girl routine."

"Might work, but might not. If he's on the run ... you know."

"That would suck, and my feelings would be hurt. Okay, option two it is. Toast this for me would you. And don't let Roscoe steal it. She handed him her stick and walked away. She was soon back, carrying a huge tree over her shoulder. It was dripping water as it had fallen in the river during a previous storm. She dumped it across the roadway then returned for her hot dog. He was staring at her wide eyed.

"What? I didn't rip it out by the roots, it was fallen across the river."

"I know, I saw it earlier."

"I have to admit, Jack. You're pretty cool under fire. Nothing I've done so far has scared you."

"Oh it's scared me all right. I just haven't let you see it."

"I won't hurt you."

"I know." Her upraised eyebrow brought a smile to his face. "Roscoe. To earn the kind of trust you have with him speaks of a gentle spirit, not a violent person."

"I can, and sometimes do, resort to violence."

"Last resort, I'll bet." He grinned and nodded at Roscoe who was eyeing her breakfast.

"Yeah, it is. My father's a violent man. I don't want to be like him." He nodded and returned his gaze to the fire.

Suddenly she sat up straight. "Here he comes. You go stand by the tree and I'll hide."

"Hide, why?"

"In case he runs. I'll stop him. I won't hurt him, Jack, but I'll make him listen." He nodded and she hid in the trees by the roadside.

A car came around the curve too fast. It nearly rolled over trying to get stopped before crashing into the tree. Once stopped, the driver threw it into reverse and hit the gas. The engine screamed, but the car didn't move. Wide eyed, the driver finally noticed the man standing by the tree, grinning at him. He took his foot off the gas and stuck his head out the window. "Jack, is that you?"

"It's me, Jimmy. Shut off the car."

"What? Why?"

"Look in the mirror." He did and blanched. There was a young white girl standing behind the car and it was tilted. She was obviously holding it up. "Turn the car off. She's getting tired and she'll flip it on the roof in a minute. Turn it off."

He did and Lenora set it down. "All right you two, talk to each other. I'm gonna call my girlfriend." She pulled out her phone as she walked away.

Lenora gave them an hour after finishing her conversation with Heather. She walked over to them, grabbed the roadblock then hauled it out of the way. "All good here, Jack?"

"Getting there, Seeker." He pulled a wad of cash from the pocket of his jacket. "Here's the money." Lenora peeled off a couple of hundreds and passed the rest back. "Get going boys. Run free."

"Seeker?"

"You owe me one, Jack Longtree, and I will collect one day."

She was nearly to the camper when his voice stopped her. "Seeker." She stopped and looked back. "It was an honor. Run free." She smiled and climbed aboard her camper.

"Who, no what, the hell was that?" asked Jimmy.

"Not sure. Wendigo maybe, but I don't think so. Bounty Hunter for sure. Calls herself the Seeker. Think I'll call her sister." Jimmy nodded then climbed back into his car. Jack joined him. They sped away in a different direction.

Lenora drove for an hour then pulled over. She called Heather just to hear her voice. "Hi pretty lady."

"Hi yourself, sweet woman. You on your way back?"

"I was."

"Lennie?"

"It went too easy. Something's not right, and my intuition is driving me crazy."

"Did you do the job?"

"Yeah."

"Get paid?"

"Yeah."

"But?"

"I like the guy, Heather. He feels like family. His brother didn't."

"Go on then, my love, check it out. Be careful too. I want you back in one piece."

"I will, sweetie. I will. I won't spend a lot of time on this either. It's just that something feels wrong."

"Okay, but call me ... lots?"

"I promise."

Lenora closed the connection then stepped out of the van. She closed her eyes and focused on Jack. She found him easily, bound and gagged in the trunk of his brother's car. "Shit. I knew it was too easy." She turned the camper around and headed back. It was dark before she caught up with them.

They were in an old cabin, not visible from the road. It was a lonely spot. Jack was lying on his side on the floor while his brother worked his way through a bottle of whiskey.

"It's your own goddamned fault, Jack. You couldn't just leave off, go play cops and robbers, leave me alone. Fuck, all my life I've had to put up with you. Pain in the goddamned ass." He picked up the syringe from the table, tied off his arm, then injected himself. A moment later he sighed and relaxed.

"If you hate me, why did you pay my way through school?"

"I hoped it would keep you away from me. How does it feel, super cop? Knowing it was drug money that put you through college? Shit. You know what, we're not even brothers, we can't be. Dad must have found you on the streets of the city. He brought you home, made up that story about you being his son. You're just some white guy's bastard kid from some old whore." He tossed back another glass of whiskey.

"You know what else? I'm sick of running from you. Three fucking years. That's how long I've been running from you. Three years and you never managed to get the feds off your trail. Some super cop you are."

"Don't do this, Jimmy. Dad's still alive. He calls me once a week asking if I found you yet. Am I bringing you home?"

"Oh sure, back to the res. There's a step up in the world. Fuck that. I'm going to crack your skull for being so fucking stupid, and then I'm going to set this place on fire with you in it. That's what I'm going to do."

"No you're not," said a soft feminine voice from the shadows.

Jimmy spun around, a gun in his hand. She was standing in the doorway. "You! Get your white ass in here."

Lenora obliged, but a lot faster than he expected. She leaped from the doorway, tore the gun from his hand and had him in a sleeper hold. He flailed about for a moment then relaxed. She lowered him to the floor then cut Jack's bonds. "Why'd you come back?"

"It just didn't feel right, Jack. I'm really sorry it worked out this way, but I'm glad I got here in time."

"Yeah, me too." He grinned ruefully. "So, now what? What are you going to do with him?"

"He's wanted by the feds, right? I'll hand him over to them."

"They'll kill him, torture him first for information about his connections, then they'll kill him."

"The man's a killer and a drug dealer, Jack. I can't let him go."

"I know, Seeker." He reached over and took the gun from her hand. With sad eyes he turned and put a bullet through the man's heart. "Better from a brother than from those men. This way I can tell Dad he's at peace finally."

She didn't respond, warring inside. She'd just witnessed a man shoot his own brother to keep him from being tortured. "He spent years in the drug business. I thought he was in the military, but he was in the drug trade. He caused a lot of misery, Seeker, and he suffered for it too. Now he's at peace and can't hurt anybody anymore."

Lenora came to the conclusion that Jack had actually done the right thing under the circumstances. "Leave his car here. I'll drop you off somewhere, anywhere you want. You found him in a burned out cabin. Dead, probably fell asleep while drunk and accidentally burned the place down."

"You're not going to turn me in?"

"No, I'm not, you did right. Come on, Jack, let's go." She led him outside then lit the barbecue with the spare propane tank sitting on it. They were halfway back to the road when the propane blew. They could hear the roar of the flames as they walked away.

"So, where to?" They'd just gotten back into the camper and Roscoe had elected to ride in Jack's lap.

"Someplace where I can catch a bus I guess."

"What'll you do now, Jack?"

"Head back to the res. They have their own cops now; I'll see if I can join up."

"You'll be a good one." Lenora drove through the night then put him on a bus for his home reservation. He'd tried to give her the rest of the money, but she refused.

It was late afternoon when she stepped through the door of the office. Heather took one look at her and leaped to her feet. "Lenora, when did you sleep last?"

"Couple of days ago I think."

"Sweet Jesus, Lennie. Oh my god." She was holding Lenora tightly and fighting back tears. "Uncle Morty ..."

"Go on, Heather, take her home. Feed her then make her sleep for a week. Go."

Heather needed no further urging. She practically dragged Lenora out to the camper. She took the keys, put Lenora in the bunk then drove away.

A Paying Job

Lenora awakened in the bunk of her camper, Heather beside her, reading. "Well, there's life after all, Roscoe." The dog jumped up and started nuzzling at Lenora.

"Okay, okay, I'm awake. Roscoe, quit it. Heather, help me."

Laughing, Heather rescued her from the squirming dog. "Hungry?"

"Starved. How long was I out?"

"Sixteen hours. Do your business while I cook breakfast. Roscoe and I went grocery shopping."

"Oh yeah? Cool. You get lots of hot dogs, Roscoe?"

"Lenora, you have to eat something else besides hot dogs."

"Tell that to Roscoe, he does the shopping."

"Ha, ha, ha, Miss Funny Bones."

Heather soon had bacon and eggs cooking on the tiny stove. Lenora emerged from the bathroom, looking freshly scrubbed and wide awake. She stepped outside, faced the sun which was now high in the sky, said a prayer to Moragah, then returned. She put her arms around Heather and nuzzled her neck. "Mmm, you smell good."

"That's bacon you smell. Sit now and we'll have breakfast at noon."

Lenora dove in and didn't speak until her plate was clean. "Oh gods, that was delicious. I'm keeping you."

Heather grinned at her and patted her hand. "That's the plan."

"So, did you find us a home?"

"Sadly, not yet. Not many places will accept pets, and we're not parting with Roscoe."

"No ma'am, we surely are not. So, what's the plan?"

"I don't have one, Lennie. I was waiting for you to get back so we could work it out together."

Lenora nodded. "You get the car back to Mary Jo okay?"

"I did. She's such a sweetheart. When she found out you were gone on a job she insisted I stay for dinner. She would have asked me to stay the night, but her B&B was full."

"That's great to hear. Now, talk to me, pretty lady. You've got something on your mind."

"Oh, it's nothing really. Just a silly dream."

"Talk to me, woman."

"The place next door to Mary Jo is for sale. It was set up as a dog kennel, but the couple divorced before they could get it up and running."

"You'd like to do that someday, wouldn't you?"

"Yeah, I would. Don't go crazy on me now. I know you believe in living on the cash at hand program."

"I do, yes. I've seen what happens to folks when the banks get the hooks into them. Not going there. Not ever. Having said that, the idea of buying a small place somewhere is kind of appealing."

"Oh, B.S.. I know you better than that. You're a natural nomad."

"But you're not, are you?"

"I can adapt."

"What's going on in that pretty noggin of yours?"

Heather sighed and began studying her hands. "I just about went nuts the last few times you've been away. I hate it that you won't take care of yourself. I know you get focused on the job and forget everything else, and I know this last time you drove all night just to get back to me sooner."

"Heather, are you saying what I think you're saying?"

"Uncle Morty can handle both businesses, Lennie. That life was never my choice and I ... I want to come with you when you're on the job. I want to be there to make sure you rest, have clean clothes, eat, etc. I want to be there to care for you. Look, I know it can be dangerous. I'll stay well back out of the action. I know I don't have super powers, and I'm not the risk taker type. I'm a nurturer. You and Roscoe need me. Please say yes. Please."

"There's just one thing."

"What's that?"

"We'll need a bigger camper, a small motor home maybe. Something with a trailer hitch so we can pull your car along with us."

Heather practically leaped into Lenora's arms. "You mean it, Lennie? You'll take me with you?"

"I'd like nothing better, pretty lady. Shall we go shopping for a motor home?"

"I want to talk to Uncle Morty first."

"He's going to shoot me."

"Come on, tough bounty hunter, I'll protect you."

They walked into the office hand in hand. There was a couple there with Morty. One look told Lenora these folks had money and lots of it. She could also tell they were desperate. Something big was up.

Morty took one look at Heather then sighed. He shot Lenora a look then introduced his guests. "This Mr. and Mrs. Galager of North Bay. Mr. and Mrs. Galager, this is my niece, Heather, and this is Lady Seeker. She's the bounty hunter you want to talk to."

The woman looked at Lenora and her skepticism was easy to read. The man just looked hopeful. "Okay, how can I help you folks?"

It was the man who spoke. "It's about our daughter."

"She's been captured by a cult," said the woman.

The man gave his wife an exasperated look. "That's not quite accurate. Lisa joined the cult, of her own free will. However, they've refused to allow us to see her, and we believe she's being kept against her will."

"So you already know where she is. Why do you need me?"

"The chief of police in North Bay is a friend. He recommended we consult a rather exclusive private detective agency ..."

"And Seline Elmore sent you to me."

"Yes. She said if anyone could bring Lisa home it would be you."

"All right, first things first. Is there an active police warrant out on your daughter?"

The woman was offended immediately. "What? No, of course not. How can you even suggest such a thing?"

Lenora didn't respond to her tone; she just went on calmly. "That presents a problem. Look, folks, I won't bring anyone back against their will unless there's an active warrant. That's called kidnapping, and I won't go there."

"What if she wants to come home?"

"Well, sir, I get that some of these cults can be pretty controlling, and I understand that she might say one thing when she's afraid to say another. However, I'll know the difference. If I go after her, but she refuses to come with me and means it, I won't bring her back."

The woman didn't even try to hide her contempt. "In that case you won't be paid."

"Okay, I guess that concludes our business then." Lenora turned away and poured a cup of coffee.

"Emily, just shut the hell up, will you. Seeker, I know in my heart my daughter wants to come home. Name your fee."

Lenora took a sip of her coffee, her eyes boring into the woman who looked away. "Fifty thousand up front. Another fifty if she comes out with me."

"What??? That's outrageous."

"Dammit, Emily, just stay out of this. All right, Seeker, you've got a deal. When can you leave?" He was already writing the check.

"As soon as the check clears."

"What? Now just a minute ..."

"Sorry folks, but Morty can tell you, I work for cash. I don't trust banks, and I don't trust checks. As soon as the check clears I'll locate Lisa and get on the road."

He stuffed his checkbook back into his suit pocket. "There's a bank across the street. I'll be right back." He strode purposefully out of the office.

Lenora turned to the wife. "So, Lisa's your stepdaughter, right?"

"You could tell?"

Lenora chuckled. "Yeah, I could tell. Let me guess. Spoiled little rich girl, apple of daddy's eye, didn't approve of the second marriage, and probably ran off with the cultists to cause as much fuss as possible."

"In a nutshell." The woman sighed deeply, softening at last. "You read people well, Seeker."

"Yeah. It's part of what I do."

"You set your fee high because you don't really want the job, didn't you?"

Lenora drained her coffee cup. "Busted. You read people pretty well too."

"Yes, well James has called your bluff, girl. Here he comes now."

Lenora sighed. "No rest for the wicked. Heather, honey ..."

"I'll hit the grocery store, then pack." She smiled and hurried out the door just as Mr. Galager returned.

"Here it is, fifty thousand. Count it."

"No need, I trust you, Mr. Galager."

"When can you start?"

"Now is as good a time as any. Got a picture of the lady for me?" He passed her a photo of a college age girl, smiling primly at the camera. Lenora nodded and studied the picture for a moment. She then closed her eyes and began to talk softly. "All right, Lisa Galager, talk to me, sweetie. Tell me where you're ... ah, there you are. Ah shit. Don't worry, honey, I'll get you out of there."

"What the hell are you doing?" asked the wife.

"I'm psychic, that's how I find people. That's why I don't spend weeks tracking them down."

"Miss Elmore did say you could find anybody anywhere."

"Nothing but the truth. Sir, I'm pretty sure Lisa will be more than happy to come home."

"Oh thank god. What did you see?"

"She's dressed in some sort of long gown. They've shaved her head, and they all were all praying to a guy standing up with his arms raised. She sure didn't look happy. Nope, Lisa Galager isn't feeling the rapture. She's in a ranch house, sort of a compound, about a day and a half northwest from here. But you knew this already."

"Yes. The ranch is on Indian land, and they wouldn't let us pass. Will that stop you?"

"Nope. Could be a nuisance, but it won't stop me. As soon as Heather gets back I'll head out."

"Is there a contract to sign?"

"Handshake." Lenora grinned and stuck out her hand. "Relax, it's a verbal agreement. Morty's an officer of the court and he witnessed the whole thing." She tossed the bag of money to Morty. "Can you put that in the safe until I get back?"

"Sure, Seeker. I take it Heather's going with you."

"I'll keep her safe, Morty, I swear I will."

"You'd better." He stepped into the back room then returned a few minutes later. Mr. Galager visibly relaxed to see that she wasn't about to run off with his money and disappear.

At that point Heather came hurrying in. "Okay, larder's topped up. I just need to grab a change of clothes or two." She hurried through the office and disappeared. A few minutes later she returned with an overnight bag. "Okay, are we good to go?"

"I just need a contact number." Mr. Galager handed her a business card with a different number on the back. "All right, we're good to go." Lenora took Heather's hand and led her out the door.

They'd been on the road for a while. Heather was being quiet, just watching the world roll by. "You okay, sweetie? Having second thoughts?"

"What? No. No, no, no. Are you?"

"Not a one. It's just that you've been so quiet."

"Sorry. I was just reflecting on life."

"Heavy stuff. Care to share your thoughts?"

"My life's changed so much in the past year, Lennie. So much. A year ago I was in school, dreaming of the day I could be a vet in a small town somewhere. I could earn a living, pay off my student debt, pay back my dad, and hopefully, before I turned forty, get a small place of my own, maybe meet someone nice, start a family, and get the mortgage paid off before I reached retirement age.

"Then Mom and Dad got killed and suddenly I was a business woman."

"Not a good fit?"

"Not even close. I was just about to jump off a bridge when you appeared on the scene, worked your magic, and made all my debts go away. Uncle Morty took me under his wing, started to train me to do the job that fate insisted I do ..."

"But, as pretty as you are in that blue suit ..."

"It doesn't feel right, Lennie. It feels like someone else's shoes. That business was Dad's dream, not mine."

"Still want to be a vet?"

"That wasn't the dream either."

"Oh?"

"I love animals and I wanted a way to be able to help them and still support myself. I like people too, but I wanted to spend my days with people who love animals as much as I do. Being a vet seemed like the only answer. The only one that would let me pay off the debts at least.

"Now, one year later, here I am, in love with a girl who has super powers, hangs out with dragons, and lives like a nomad."

"Still a long way from the dream, isn't it sweetie?" Lenora was smiling gently, still focused on the road ahead. "Is it so bad?"

"No, my love, not bad, just different. I'm actually feeling like a weight has been lifted off my shoulders. I know Uncle Morty's disappointed, but he'll understand. He knows deep inside the business wasn't for me."

"Do you owe him any money?"

"What? No, no, that's all square. I've got a few hundred left, but at least I'm out of debt."

"That's the key, sweet Heather, that's the key."

"The key? Lennie, what does that mean, the key?"

"The key to freedom, the key to a happy life. Being debt free is the key."

"Okay, I've been whining about my stuff too long. Now I'm going back to poking into your stuff. Talk to me, sweet woman."

"About what?" Lenora was grinning.

"Let's start with why you always insist on being paid in cash. Why you don't trust banks. What's that all about?"

"My father was a violent man, this you already knew. No matter how bad or how often he beat her, my mother would never leave him. I asked her once and she said we couldn't afford it. We'd have no place to live, we'd be on the street.

"They both worked, my parents, big mortgage, car loans, home improvement loans, etc. The more we owed the bank, the more often he went nuts. It was the stress and frustration that set him off much of the time. Yeah, he took it out on us, but it was the stress that set him off. No matter how hard they tried, my parents just seemed to fall deeper and deeper into debt.

"There was a family just down the street from us who got foreclosed on. Just like that, one day you have a home to go to, the next you're on the sidewalk in front of what used to be your house, watching as the bank rep and the real estate guy put a For Sale sign on the lawn and have your car towed away. Not going to happen to me."

"Do you think we'll ever have a real home? Not right now, but someday, do you think we could ... Oh my god, that's why you set your fee so high for this job, isn't it?"

"Yeah, it is. Those folks can afford it. That guy has banker written all over him."

"He's a banker?"

"Oh, I don't know, but that's the level he plays at. He can pay me and not even notice the loss. You saw how fast he went across the street and came back with a bag of money. Heather, when you said the place next to Mary Jo was empty and for sale, did you get the price?"

"No. Lennie, what are you saying here?"

"I'm saying I have no objections at all to us owning a home, as long as we own it, not the banks. Penny and Tara have a great little condo. Tasha and Kara live with the soldiers on the streets and in the sewer hideout and they're happy. Seline and Ellen are rich by any standards. The point is, they've all managed to find a way to have a home and still do what Moragah needs them to do. If we find a little place to raise dogs and chickens, I'm all for that."

"But we live on the cash system? That's why the hot dogs, old camper van, you're saving up?"

"Not exactly, sweetie. The hot dogs are because me and Roscoe like 'em. The van is because, at the time, it was what I could afford. I started saving up when you told me about that place being for sale."

"Lennie, I didn't mean to sound like I was demanding you buy it for me."

"I know, but you sure sounded wistful when you spoke of it."

"Yes I did, and I need a kick in the butt for that. Lennie, hear me. I want to be with you. I'll be happy as a puppy in this camper, if you're here too. This job of yours will keep us on the move, and I want to be on the move with you. Can we put off the house and white picket fence for a decade or two?"

Heather smiled at Lenora's delighted laugh. "Yes, pretty lady, we can put it back for a few years. I'll confess, I enjoy the freedom of the nomad lifestyle. We should get a bigger camper though."

"I agree. I'll need a couple of square feet for an office."

"Office?"

"I learned enough about business in the last few months to know how to keep the tax man at bay. Might as well put that to work. I'll be the business manager, you be the Seeker, and Roscoe will be the muscle."

Lenora was grinning. "Deal. Uh-oh, is that a beagle doing the pee pee dance back there?"

Heather turned to see Roscoe dancing around by the door. "Looks like you're right on that one."

Lenora pulled over by a stand of trees and Heather let Roscoe out. A moment later loving arms encircled her waist. "It's getting late, pretty lady. Want to call it a day?"

"Yeah, let's do. You keep an eye on our enforcer while I cook dinner."

"Have I told you today that I love you?"

"Yeah, yeah, you just love it that I'm so domestic."

"Not just, my sweet, but it is on the top ten list." Heather laughed, poked her in the ribs with a finger, then climbed back into the camper and started cooking. Roscoe finished his business then jumped in the camper, reappeared with his tug toy, and wagged his tail at Lenora. They were still at it when Heather called them in.

Next morning Roscoe snuffled around, carefully choosing, and then anointing the proper tree, while the girls said their morning prayer to Moragah. After that came a hearty breakfast and then they set out again. The sun was nearly down when they arrived at the barricade in the road. They'd reached the reservation. Armed men stood in the road, one holding up a hand to stop them. Lenora turned off the van and got out.

"Afternoon, fellas, how's it going?"

"You can't camp here; this is tribal land."

"Wasn't looking to camp, boys, just stopped to say hello."

"You've said it, now turn around and get out of here."

"Love to, but there's a small problem."

"Fuck this. I said get going."

The big man took a step toward her, leveling a shotgun. Lenora moved. Suddenly the man was on his ass with the shotgun pointed at his temple. Several rifles were pointed at her. "Drop the guns, boys. Drop 'em or I'll blow his brains all over this dust bowl then come after you."

A large woman stepped toward her. "What the hell are you doing, bitch?" She reached to grab Lenora, but a fist cracked against her jaw and she sank to the ground, unconscious.

"Don't call me bitch. I don't like it. Are those guns down or do I dust this guy?"

At that point a car arrived and two men got out. The older man went for his gun, but the other stopped him. "No Donnie, no. Let me. Everybody put your guns down. Now! Do not piss off the white girl. Bad things happen when she gets mad."

"I can believe that," grunted the man on the ground.

"Hey there, Seeker."

"Hi Jack, how's it going?"

"About average."

"How's you Dad?"

"He took it hard, but he'll be okay. Can I have that shotgun?"

"Are those guys going to shoot me?"

"Nope."

"All right." Lenora spun the shotgun and passed it to him so it was pointing at her. She offered her hand to the man on the ground to help him up. "You okay?"

"I'll live." There was a groan from the ground and he bent to help the woman up. They moved away and the older man with Jack stepped closer.

"Seeker, is that what he called you? The bounty hunter?"

"Yep, that's me."

"I'm Donnie Runningbull. I'm the law here. I don't care what warrants you have. They're no good here."

"I'm not after one of your people, Sheriff. I'd have come straight to you if I was."

"So why are you here?"

"I'm not here to cause trouble, trespass on your land, or anything else like that. I'm just here for one person. There's a ranch house just over that hill with a bunch of crazies in it. I expect they pay you well to keep the busybodies away. Trouble is, one of them wants to leave and her daddy has paid me to make that happen."

"Can't let you do that."

"Can't stop me, Sheriff. I came up the road as a sign of respect. I could have come in overland, killed the lot of them, and taken my girl out. I didn't. I came respectfully because of Jack. What did he tell you about me?"

"A lot of bullshit and whiskey talk."

"Jack doesn't drink, and you know it. Just because you didn't want to hear what he said doesn't make him a liar, it makes you a fool."

He didn't rise to that bait. "Well, you took Tommy's shotgun and decked Aleta. I guess some of it must have been true at that, but Wendigo?"

She looked at Jack and he winked. She turned back to the sheriff. "Test me and find out."

"Don't do it, Donnie," said the man who she'd taken the shotgun from.

The sheriff sighed. "Miss, this presents a problem here. Tribal law says no one steps on tribal land without an escort. Our people have a treaty with those people. We're supposed to protect them."

"And you can do that. Come with me, keep them out of my way while I pick up my target. That way they'll survive another day."

"Can't do it. I can't."

"Fine, then I'll do it the hard way." Lenora turned and walked back to her van. They all gasped and fell silent when she spoke. "Heather, turn the van around and go back to that town about two hours away. Go into the sheriff's office and wait there for me."

"Lennie?"

"This is how it is, Heather. Some days it's easy and some days it's like this. Go on now. I need to know you're safe."

Lenora heard Jack's voice behind her. "Donnie, you dumb bastard, you've just gotten all these people killed. Run, people, run while you can."

"Stop. Just a fucking minute here. Just stop, everybody. Seeker, wait a minute."

"I'm losing daylight here, Sheriff."

"Look, if what you say is true, that your target wants to come out, I'll talk to these people myself. I'll take you up there and we'll get to the bottom of this."

"All right, I'll go with you, but understand. No matter what, I'm bringing Lisa out with me."

"Take the offer, Donnie."

"Jack, if you're lying about ..."

Jack stepped up to Lenora then turned. Raising his voice, he spoke to the whole gathering. "I claim this woman as my sister. Full blood sister. If any harm comes to her or her woman I'll personally hunt and kill the one responsible. You all know me. Think hard about what I say."

Lenora quirked an eyebrow at him. "Sister?"

"Well, I can't marry you, you've got a wife in the car."

"Good point. So, Sheriff, what's it going to be?"

"We go, now."

"Jack, you stay here and keep an eye out for Heather."

"You sure, Seeker?"

"I'm sure. Tommy, bring that shotgun and come with us. The sheriff might need back up."

"Remember what I said," called Jack as they climbed into the sheriff's car.

"I know, I know," muttered big Tommy, "don't piss off the white girl." Lenora grinned.

The car spun around and raced away. A few minutes later it pulled up to the door of the ranch house.

A tall thin man stepped out then closed the door behind him. "What are you doing here? The next payment's not due until Tuesday."

"I'm not here for money. This woman wants to talk to ..."

"I'm here for Lisa Galager."

Lenora stepped towards the house, but the man blocked her path. "We don't allow nobody to talk to the women. Get out of here, now."

Lenora grabbed him and tossed him. He landed in a heap several feet away. Before anyone could react she kicked in the door and was inside. The sheriff and Tommy just looked at each other as they heard the shots and screams. They started towards the door, but there was a sudden rush of people fleeing the house, some screaming, some sobbing, and a few bleeding.

A minute later Lenora reappeared carrying a sobbing girl in her arms. She went to the car and got in the back seat with the girl still in her arms. "Hush now, it's okay, Lennie's got you. We're going home now."

If there was any doubt in the sheriff's mind it vanished with the girl's answer. She stopped and sniffed. "You really mean that? You'll take me home?"

"Yes I will, honey. I will. My girl Heather is in the camper. We'll go there first, get you something decent to wear, some real food, and then we'll head for home."

The sheriff started toward the car, but a shot rang out. Tommy started to swear as blood spurted from his arm. Both he and the sheriff dove for cover. Lenora was out of the car in a heartbeat. There was a crash as a big window exploded inward. A scream of pain followed, and then a body came flying through the window, arms flailing until he crashed into the side of the car. He fell to the ground moaning and groaning.

A few more howls of pain came from the house, followed closely by two running men, and lastly by Lenora. She stood in the broken doorway and shouted. "That does it. Now I'm pissed off. This ends now. If any of you assholes start up again I'll kill the lot of you and burn the bodies. Sheriff, start the damn car. Lisa wants to go home." She got back in the car and enfolded the girl in her arms.

"You okay, Tommy?"

"Yeah, I'm good, Sheriff. Jack was right. Don't piss off the white girl."

The sheriff chuckled at that. "You got that right. So, Wendigo, what happens now?"

"Now we go away, Sheriff. I got what I came for. Now I take her home to her family. I didn't come here to cause you trouble. I didn't want to hurt anybody. I just wanted to take Lisa home. If you had just let me in and those fools had let me take her without a fuss then no harm done. As it is, I beat up poor old Tommy here, made Jack adopt me, and I made a complete mess out of that bunch of morons up there.

"You can write it up this way. A group of nut jobs were working up a big ceremony and it got away from them. A wendigo came and tore them up before vanishing with a sacrificial virgin." Tommy and the sheriff laughed at that. Even Lisa giggled a bit.

When they got back to the barricade there was a party going on. Everybody was standing around a fire roasting hotdogs. Including Heather. "Hey now, where did those hot dogs come from?"

"Your van," grinned Jack.

"What? Heather, tell me you didn't give these people all the hot dogs."

"I tried to save you one, honey, but Roscoe got it."

"Aw, now that really sucks. I'm out there, getting shot at, saving the maiden, and you guys eat all my hot dogs."

Jack grinned and passed her a roasted hot dog on a stick. "Don't cry, sis, I saved you one." He passed her another and she passed it to Lisa who took it with wide eyes.

"Heather, this is Lisa. She's on her way home so I said she could ride with us for a couple of days."

"Nice to meet you, Lisa. You're about my size. Come into the camper with me. We'll get you into some jeans and a tank top."

Heather led the girl away and Lenora turned back to the gathering. "So, everything's good here?"

"Yeah, all good here," said one man. "That girl of your sure can cook."

"Aw come on, don't tell me you guys ate me out of house and home." There was a round of laughter at that.

"Hey, Wendigo, anybody left alive up there?"

"Yeah, they're fine. I went easy on them. You know, didn't want to make a mess on brother Jack's home turf and all."

"You're a hard woman, my sister. A hard woman." Jack grinned as he passed her another hot dog. The fun and banter around the fire went on for a while then Lenora loaded Heather and Lisa into the van and left.

"Lennie, are you really mad at me for feeding those folks?"

"No, sweetie, not at all. It was well done. You made us some new friends and allies. Even if those crazies try to kick up a fuss because of what I did, those folks will block it. Besides, you showed them respect and friendship. They don't see a lot of that from us white folks. I'm actually quite proud of the way you handled that."

Heather beamed her a smile then turned to Lisa. "So, how long were you with ..."

"The cult? Three months. At first it was exciting, but once Michael got me to the compound it changed. He didn't want me anymore. He gave me to one of the other men." She burst into tears and Heather slipped out of the seat and went to gather the distraught girl into her arms.

Eventually she cried herself to sleep. She was on the bunk so Heather pulled a blanket over her then returned to the passenger's seat. "Are you planning to drive all night?"

"No, not really, but I want to put some distance between us and those idiots back there. We'll bypass the first town, but we'll take a motel room at the next one, get some rest, then move out from there. You want to call the client and let them know we're on our way?"

Heather pulled out her phone and thumbed it on. She made the call and a moment later it was answered. "Mr. Galager, this is Heather Jones of Seeker, Inc. Sir, the mission was successful and we're on our way back. Lisa is sleeping now, but as soon as she wakes I'll have her call you. Yes, she's fine, sir. All went well, no worries. Yes, goodbye, Mr. Galager."

They stopped for the night and the next day they took Lisa shopping for clothes. Another night in a motel and then they were back at Morty's office. It was just before noon. Lisa stepped through the door and flew into her father's arms. To Emily's surprise the girl reached for her and pulled her into the hug too. The woman looked over the top of Lisa's head to make eye contact with Lenora who just grinned and winked at her.

Mr. Galager gently released himself from the embrace and placed a briefcase on the desk. "Here's your fee, Seeker. It's all there, count it if you like."

"I trust you." Lenora poured herself a coffee. "Take her home now folks. Lisa's had a rough time of it lately, but she's tougher than she looks."

"I'm not the only one," replied the girl, as she reached for and squeezed Lenora's hand.

"Remember what I told you."

"Life's not fair, but if it doesn't kill you it makes you stronger."

"That's the ticket, girl. Have a good life, Lisa. Stay strong."

"Run free, Lady Seeker." With that, they left the office and Lenora sank into a chair.

Heather patted her shoulder. "Honey, could you take all that cash and put it in the bank. I want a few minutes with Uncle Morty."

"Sure, I can do that." Morty got the rest of her money from the safe and passed it to her. "Morty, I kept her safe like I promised." He just nodded and she left for the bank.

Heather watched her go then, smiling warmly, turned to Morty. "I'm really sorry, Uncle Morty. I am. I wanted it to work out, I did, but ..."

"I know, Heather, I know. You were never cut out for this business. I'll hire somebody for the other office. Please, just promise you'll stay safe. I have no real idea how she does what she does, but it scares me. Lenora goes up against the toughest there are, and sooner or later one of them will get lucky, and I don't want you in the line of fire when that happens."

"Listen to this. We were at the barricade in the road. It looked like it was getting messy. Lennie told me to turn the van around, go back to the nearby town, and wait for her in the sheriff's office."

"Really?"

"Truly."

"So what happened? Did you go?"

"Didn't need to. They suddenly realized she meant business. Their sheriff went with her to help rescue the girl, and I got out the hot dogs. The rest of us had a bonfire and weenie roast while they were gone. I made a bunch of new friends and Lennie did the nasty. I was a mile or more away from the action.

"She loves me, Uncle Morty. She won't let anything happen to me, and I'm not the type to insist on getting into the fight with her. That's Lennie's job."

Morty sighed and sank into his chair. "Well, okay I guess. As long as you stay out of the action."

"I will. I'm the cook, nag, and nurturer, as well as the business manager. Lennie is the Seeker, the bounty hunter, the warrior."

Morty sighed again, accepting his fate. There was no arguing with a woman in love and he knew it. At that point, Lenora returned from the bank. "Everything cool here?"

"Yeah, we're good, Lennie," said Morty.

"Oh, hey, I've just had a great idea." Heather's enthusiasm brought a smile to both Lenora and Morty. "Listen to this. Uncle Morty, if this works for you it would be perfect. Let me use that same desk as before. I can keep Lennie's books up to date, act as her receptionist, and still help you with the business when we're in town. You get some help and Lennie gets to see me in that navy suit that she likes so much. What'd ya think?"

"I think you're both crazy, but sure. It works for me. I get a bit of help, a bounty hunter working out of my office, and Lennie can stop using me as her banker. I expect you two to pick up the tab for the coffee."

"I get to see Heather in that navy job once in a while? Hey, I'm in." Heather beamed her delight. "You can do the suit tomorrow sweetie, today we have to go hunting for a new house on wheels." She took Heather by the hand and led her out the door.

Morty shook his head as they left. "First they take over your life, then they take over your office. Maybe it's time I got married. Some tough old broad who can defend me from those two." He was chuckling to himself as he went back to work.

Heather and Lenora got quite a surprise as they inspected the range of possibilities in new motor homes. Some were positively luxurious. Eventually they gave up and drove away.

"Didn't see anything you liked, sweetie?"

"I liked all of them. The problem is, for what one of those costs, we could buy a small place, have a home, and take this camper when we're out of town. I don't even want to think what it would cost to fill the tank on one of those monsters."

Lenora chuckled. "Oh girl, you've been hanging out with me too long."

Heather laughed with delight. "Maybe, but as gorgeous as they are, I smell money pit. Let's not rush. Let's just wait and see what the world has to offer. After all, we're just ..." Her phone began to ring. "Hello, Uncle Morty, what's up? Okay, we're on our way."

"Another job?"

"Yeah, and he's pissed. He took a chance on this kid."

"Okay, let's head back. You hit the grocery store and I'll pick up the paperwork on this guy."

You Can Run

They'd been on the road for three days and were no closer to their quarry. The kid had stolen a motorcycle and run. "As long as he keeps moving on that damn crotch rocket we'll never catch him."

Heather was driving and she reached over to pat Lenora's thigh. "Don't fuss, sweetie. We'll catch him. He can't run forever."

"Yeah, I guess. I'm just pissed that we'll spend the whole bounty on gas trying to catch this bird."

"Maybe we need to change tactics. Figure out where he's going and head him off."

"Why not. Find us a place to pull over, we'll stretch our legs and see if Roscoe has any better ideas. I'm starting to wonder about this guy."

"Oh?"

"Yup. I think he knows who's after him. He knows the only way to stay out of my clutches is to keep moving and moving fast."

"How could he know that?"

"Morty probably told him not to run or I'd go after him. Morty seems quite happy to have an in house Bounty Hunter. That was good thinking on your part."

"Thank you, thank you, now, here's a spot to stretch our legs."

They took Roscoe for a run and when they returned Heather started cooking while Lenora went for a super run. She returned soaked in sweat and breathing heavily. "I've got to start training again. I'm out of shape."

"Ah-huh. Here, have some water then eat before you shower. Then we can plot strategy. I have an idea how we can gain on this guy."

"Oh yeah? Do tell."

"Nope, I want you to clean up and put on that dress. Once you're feeling like a girl again instead of a frustrated warrior, then I'll talk."

"In the words of brother Jack, you're a hard woman, Heather Jones."

"And don't you forget it. Eat up now."

"Okay, but if I'm putting on a dress ..."

"Yes, I will too. Eat." Lenora grinned and tucked in.

Lenora finished her shower, got dressed then stepped outside to find Heather in a long sun dress. "Feel better now?"

"I do, sweetie. This was a good idea. So, talk to me. What's your plan for catching this guy?"

"So far you've been doing most of the driving and I've been enjoying the scenery. You check in on him only to find he's turned off in a new direction. He did stop for one day, then took off again. Why?"

"No idea. Your best guess?"

"Exhaustion. I think he was completely worn out and had to sleep. I think the pace is killing him, and I think he's wearing down. He can't be eating or sleeping right, and he can't keep up the pace. I think it's time to push him a bit harder for a day or two until he drops then you walk in and take him in his sleep."

"Sounds good to me, pretty lady. Any idea how we can push him harder without burning out ourselves?"

"I do, actually. So far every time he changes direction he gains ground on us. We catch up a bunch while he rests, but he's on the go too soon for us to nab him. Here's the idea. I'll drive and you keep your magic eye on him. If we can change direction with him we'll cut his lead down considerably."

"I like it. Oh yeah, I like it. We could also take turns driving. One resting while the other drives, but I guess that would only work if we knew where he was going."

"Yeah, I guess."

"Pass me that map. Thanks. Okay, we first spotted him here, then he went here, and here ..." Lenora was drawing the fugitive's path while she spoke. "He's doing a lot of zig zaging, and he's doubled back on us a couple of times, but look at this."

"It looks like he's circling back to town. Look, Lennie. If we take this secondary roadway here we can get out in front of him. He's sticking to the main highways."

"Yes he is. He knows his crotch rocket can outrun anything we've got so he's staying on open road and using that speed to gain distance. All right, our turn off is about three miles from here. If we camp here, and get an early start maybe we can head him off. I'll check up on him now and see where he is."

Lenora closed her eyes and began talking to the fugitive in a soft voice. "Lenora Schmidt, such language," giggled Heather. "How un-ladylike."

Lenora laughed with her. "Stop it now, I have to focus." Again she closed her eyes and called to her quarry. She found him easily enough. He was robbing a convenience store. "Little moron just held up a store out on the highway. He was masked and on foot, but it was him. He took a few dollars in cash and some junk food. Okay, there he goes, ripping down the highway."

Heather sighed. "Maybe the police will get him."

"I doubt it. He was on foot, so they'll do a ground search first. Let me take another look." This time she turned in a different direction. "There he is, under a tree, chowing down on chips and beer. He turned back towards us. Let me see that map again." She gazed at the map for a moment. Okay, he's about right here. From where he is, there's only one likely route for him to take unless he comes right at us. If he sticks to his zig zag he'll turn off here. Your shortcut will put us right in front of him by tomorrow night.

"Roscoe, my old darling, our girlfriend sure is a smart cookie. You and I would just stay on his trail for a few months and run him down.

Good thing she's with us, huh?" The dog wagged his tail happily and tried to lick her face off while Heather laughed at them. It was good to see Lenora smiling again.

The next morning they arose early, said their morning prayer to Moragah, grabbed a quick bowl of cereal, then hit the road. Heather drove and Lenora kept checking in on the quarry. "Oh yeah, we got you, you miserable rotten son of a gun. This time we're gonna get you. He's on the right highway, Heather. You want me to drive for a while?"

"Actually, I'm getting hungry. Make me a sandwich?"

"On it." Lenora unhooked the seat belt and moved back to work. She returned with a sandwich and bottle of water for Heather. An hour later Roscoe's bladder forced a pit stop. Roscoe anointed a tree, Heather made a quick lunch for Lenora, and Lenora checked up on the fugitive. They were still on the right track.

It was late in the afternoon when they re-connected with the highway. "Find us a place to hide, pretty lady. We did it, we're ahead of him. He's coming right toward us, but not flat out. That washroom break he took a while back gave us a good lead."

Heather grinned. "Yeah, all that junk food comes with a price." They both giggled at that. "So, what's the plan now?"

"Now we wait for him to go past, then we trail him until he stops for the night. Once he's asleep I'll sneak up and grab him. I think we have time for a break. What'd ya think, Roscoe? Want to get a leg in the air? Huh? All right, let's do it."

Heather found them a pullout. Roscoe got his pee break; Lenora changed out of her dress and into boots and jeans. They ate another cold meal while waiting for the motorcycle to pass by. Once it did they let him get a mile ahead, then pulled out to follow. Heather was driving and Lenora was watching him carefully.

The sun went down and they drove on. Finally Lenora patted Heather's leg. She pulled the camper over to the shoulder of the road. A while later a silent figure slipped out of the camper and disappeared into the night. A short while after that Lenora returned, empty handed and swearing like a sailor.

"Lennie?"

"Goddam little fucker has the luck of the Irish." Lenora threw herself onto the bunk. "I was almost on him when someone's dog started barking close by. He jumped on the bike and took off like the devil was after him. Shit. Now we have to do it all over again. Find us a place for the night, sweetheart. We might as well get some sleep then dig out the map in the morning."

Heather nodded. "Roscoe, go cuddle with Lennie while I find us a pull out. She needs some puppy loving." She climbed behind the wheel and started the engine. Roscoe jumped up on the bed with Lenora who rubbed his belly. She slowly relaxed and smiled at his groans of pleasure and his wagging tail. Three days later they caught up again.

Summer was nearly over, and the evening cooled off. The haggard young man sat beside his motorcycle chewing on some beef jerky he'd stolen from a gas station earlier that day. He cursed his fate and wondered how he'd managed to mess up his life so badly. He'd just wanted the things all the other guys had. Selling drugs had seemed like the fastest way to get them. The first street sale he'd tried to make was to an under cover cop. It had been all downhill from there.

The worst part was, he hadn't believed the old fool about the bounty hunter. He should have listened. He'd spotted the old camper van behind him the second day on the road. Ever since that day it kept showing up. That damned bounty hunter was like a bloodhound. Worse yet, she had a camper. Not as fast, but it had a bed to sleep in and a toilet, as well as a place for food. Dammit, he should have stolen a camper.

His musings were cut short as he sensed something near. Listening carefully, he heard what he thought was a sound of movement in the grassy field he'd stopped in. He glanced up and saw something huge in the sky, moving towards him. Without a second thought he leaped to his feet and jumped on the bike. He heard her scream of frustration behind him as he roared away.

Lenora moved with all her speed, but she was just a breath too late. The motorcycle escaped her grasp even as the dragon landed near her. Heather had crept along behind Lenora, and she was close enough to hear her lover go someplace no sane person would ever go. She heard Lenora swearing at a demigod.

"Fuck! Godamn it to hell, Shadow, your timing truly sucks. I've been after that little shit for weeks and every time I get close he slips through my fingers. This time I had him, and then you come along and screw it all up."

The Elf showed no emotion at all as she responded to the verbal attack. "That one was your quarry?"

"He was, and now he's getting away again."

"He is not." With that the Elf leaped to the back of the dragon and the beast rose into the air to the beat of vast wings. They vanished into the night sky.

Lenora was still swearing when Heather reached her. "Easy, my love, easy. I know you're frustrated. Get a grip on that now. We don't want to annoy the Elf or dragon, now do we?"

Lenora let her shoulders slump and she grinned ruefully. "No, I guess we don't want to piss off the Elf. My bad. Guess I'll have some sucking up to do. I'll call Seline in the morning and apologize. With luck she won't feed me to the dragon."

"She's coming back."

"What?"

"There, I can see them."

"Oh shit. Quick, head for the camper. Get as far away as you can in case she's mad."

"Lennie?"

"I mouthed off to somebody I shouldn't have. There's no place to hide where she won't find me. Go on, get out of here while you can."

"No, I'm staying with you. Besides, it's too late. They're here."

Once again the dragon landed near Lenora. He looked at her then spat out his cargo. Lenora's fugitive landed in a heap at her feet. She could have sworn the beast grinned at her. The Elf dismounted and strode towards her. "Is this your quarry?"

"That's him, slippery little bugger. Look, Shadow, I ..."

"Swearing at a warrior on a dragon isn't a very good survival strategy, Seeker." This time the merriment reached the Elf's eyes. Lenora hung her head and the woman laughed. She stepped closer and took Lenora in her arms. "I do have a way of upsetting your plans, don't I, my sister?"

Lenora was chuckling too. "Like I said, your timing really sucks. So, forgive me for being a potty mouth?"

"Always. Forgive me for messing up your mojo?"

"Always, big sister."

The Elf turned to Heather. "I confess I'm somewhat disappointed in you, Heather Jones."

"Me? What did I do?"

"I had hoped you'd be a calming influence on Seeker."

"Well, I do try, but ..."

"It is a most difficult task, I'm sure."

They were all laughing now. Lenora hung her head. "Go ahead, beat me up, both of you."

Shadow smiled again. "In truth, Heather, I fully understand why she does that."

Lenora's head came up. "What do you mean?"

"Your father was a brutal man. You inherited his temper, but you channel the anger and frustration differently. You release the emotion through foul language instead of violence. As angry as you were, Heather had no fear of you. She came to you to console you."

"Sorry."

"Don't be," said Heather and Shadow in unison. They all laughed.

"Okay, all this therapy is nice, but Lady Shadow hunted me up, there must have been a reason."

"And so to business. Yes, my sister, there is a reason. You once told me you don't know what Moragah might want with a seeker. I believe I might have an idea about that.

"Listen carefully now. About a year ago, Lady Justice found something alive in the sewers of her city. She didn't know what it was, nor did Moragah. It was a creature born of hate, abuse, and toxic chemicals. Some power from the Darkness had given it the spark of life. The creature is large, fast, strong, and extremely dangerous.

"Her soldiers wanted Justice to kill it, but she didn't for it had harmed no one at that point. As time went on they discovered that it learned and absorbed information from whatever it ate. At one point a number of police went into the sewers, and in the battle that followed the beast was nearly killed. Several police officers did lose their lives, but not all the bodies were found."

"Uh-oh."

"Indeed. The creature had eaten one of those men. He then believed himself to be that man. He had his skills, intelligence, and command of language. He called himself Dan and tried to return to the officer's home. During that adventure he became aware of his true nature, but was badly wounded. Justice and Little Blue actually saved his life."

"Okay, so what has that got to do with me?"

"I'm getting there. A couple of months ago, Viper and I stopped a drug import ring and put an end to an old enemy. We had sought this man for some time. Linwood was a CIA agent, highly trained, a savage and vicious fighter, as well as a cunning opponent. A man completely without conscience, morals, or compassion. A true servant of the Dark.

"During the last battle Viper put several rounds through Linwood's heart. The man was dead, there is no doubt of that. Seeker, that battle was in a storm sewer. Linwood's body was never found."

"Oh shit."

"Exactly. I don't know what happened, but I do know that, under the influence of Justice's friendship, and the personality traits of the policeman, Dan shifted away from the Darkness. He had gained a conscience and compassion. However, he told Justice there were others like him ..."

"And if one of them has eaten your enemy ..."

"We have a monster of incredible power and evil on our hands. Can you shed any light on this?"

"Tell me all you can of this creature's physical description."

"Dan is tall, perhaps seven feet. His features are indistinct, his skin secretes some sort of acid that burns, two arms, two legs, one head. That's all I know."

Lenora nodded then closed her eyes. "Talk to me, Dan. I'm a sister to Justice, a friend. Talk to me. Where are you? Talk to me, Dan. Talk to ..." She began to sputter and choke. Her eyes flew open and she gagged again before catching her breath. Both Heather and Shadow were holding her up."

"I ask too much of you with too little to give. Forgive me, my sister. Forgive me."

Lenora leaned heavily on Heather's shoulder. "No, no. It's okay. Look, all I got was deep water. Movement through deep water. Somewhere out in the Atlantic Ocean, just off the coast. Can't be more specific. Shadow, I can tell you this. He wasn't alone."

"In your own words, oh fuck."

"What should we do?"

"There's nothing we can do at this time. We must stay alert, but that's my job. Perhaps I can convince Moragah to create a watcher to keep an eye out for him, it, or whatever. For now, let Heather take you home. I'll place your quarry under hypnosis. He'll sleep until you get him back to prison. He will awaken when you speak the magic word."

"Magic word?"

"Dragon."

"I love it."

Late the next day the young man awakened, hungry, desperate for a bathroom, and back in police custody.

Back in Training

Heather stood outside the camper, checking the time. Lenora should have been back before now. She was just starting to worry when Roscoe went on alert. A cloud of dust appeared in the distance along the old dirt road where they'd camped. Heather quickly retreated into the camper and shut the door. A moment later she heard Lenora gasping for breath, and a soft knock on the door.

"Heather, honey, it's Lennie. Let me in."

"Has the dust settled yet?"

"Almost."

"Tell me when it's settled. I know you're covered, but I just had a shower and don't want all that dust on my clothes or in my hair."

"Aw, sweetie, I'm dying of thirst out here. Don't you love me anymore?"

"I love you to bits, Silly Seeker, and I'll love you even more after you've had a shower." Heather grinned with delight to hear Lenora roar of laughter. She opened the door and passed out a bottle of water. Lenora drained it and found Heather holding out another. She drained that too.

Lenora reached for Heather as she stepped out of the van, but Heather danced away and pointed at the camper. "Shower, now."

"Yes, ma'am. Hey Roscoe, you still love me don'tcha?" He just wagged his tail and offered her the tug toy. "Sorry old buddy, Mom says I gotta clean up my act before I'm allowed to play."

Heather was smiling at both of them. "Come here, Roscoe, I'll play a game of tug o' war with you while Lennie gets a shower. Come on boy."

The dog obediently went to her and offered one end of the toy. "Oh sure, abandon me for a pretty girl with a tug toy. Fickle beast." Lenora's teasing grumble was lost in the playful growls and pulls of the game. She smiled at them then disappeared inside.

Lenora emerged later, scrubbed clean, her long hair wet and combed straight down her back, and wearing a flowing sun dress. She found Heather in a lawn chair beneath a shade tree. There was an empty chair beside her and Roscoe asleep at her feet. Lenora smiled, kissed Heather's cheek, then settled into the empty chair.

"Sweetheart, why are you pushing yourself so hard? It's been days now and you're pushing yourself harder every day. What's going on?"

"It's that damn kid on the motorcycle." Lenora sighed and took a sip of the iced tea Heather passed to her. "I should have had him."

"What do you mean?"

"He got away from me twice, the little fucker. Penny would have run him down. Crotch rocket or no, she'd have run him down and hauled him off it. Me? I needed my big sister to catch him for me."

"Are you saying Penny could outrun a motorcycle?"

"Not if he had a chance to get up to speed, maybe not, but I had him in my sights twice and he got away. I just didn't have the gas or the speed to catch him. Not going to happen again, I can tell you."

"Okay, there's more than that going on here. Talk to me, Lennie."

Lenora sighed and finished off the iced tea. "I got lazy, Heather. I got lazy and depended on the superpowers to do the job for me. Penny would have run that guy down easy, Justice would have stepped out of the wall and grabbed him, Seline ..."

"Hey, hey, no beating yourself up. You can do stuff they can't do. Even Shadow, practically a goddess in her own right, comes to you for stuff she can't do. Go easy on my girlfriend, she's a rock star and a super hero in her own right."

"Yeah, I guess."

"But?"

"But, I've been given some amazing tools to work with, and I've let them get rusty. I have to train all my abilities until they're the best they can be."

"All right, I get that, but why the sudden urgency?"

Again Lenora sighed. "Because we messed up, honey. All three of us, me, you, and Shadow."

"All three of us? Explain please."

"Shadow wanted me to locate that creature. She wants to know if that beast, or something like it took the body of her enemy."

"Yeah, so, how did we blow it?"

"She described to me, and I looked for, Dan, the creature that Justice had already influenced for the good."

"Oh crap. That's right. You should have been looking for Shadow's old enemy. Oh fuck."

"Yeah, pretty much."

"Look, Lennie, I know this is important, but I'd be a lot happier if you didn't go looking for that thing. Remember, you looked for it and couldn't breathe. I don't ..."

"It's cause it was underwater."

"What?"

"When I find someone a part of me is there with them. Now that I know they live underwater, I'll be holding my breath next time."

"Wow, I didn't know that."

"Neither did I until I damn near drowned. Anyway, that's why I'm pushing myself, pretty lady. I've got to get back in shape."

"Understood, but again I ask, why now with such urgency?"

"I have a sense that I may have to face that creature soon, or face whatever madness it could unleash on the world. I have no real evidence to support this feeling; I just want to be at my peak and ready for anything."

"Keep going."

"How do you do that? See right through me?"

"I'll tell you later. Stop trying to change the subject. Finish your thought."

"All right. I need to be at my best because I don't want you, Penny, Seline, or anybody else to get hurt because I wasn't able to hold up my end, do my job. Lady Moragah gave me amazing gifts. I need to respect that, and show her I appreciate and honor her trust in me."

Heather reached for Lenora's hand and squeezed it gently. "How can I help?"

"Just do what you do best, keep me grounded, keep me sane."

In the weeks that followed Heather located an old stone quarry where Lenora could lift and carry huge boulders from one place to the next. She dressed pretty and used her looks and smiles to keep people from noticing the dark clad figure crawling up the sides of buildings or leaping from roof to roof. She cooked, did laundry, and above all, found them paying jobs with other bondsmen. Lenora needed things and people to find.

For her part, Lenora was getting far better at her job. Physically she was in the best shape of her life and mentally she was getting clearer pictures of her targets. As well as the bounties she hunted, she also regularly went into the city and looked at the posters on the light poles. And in that time, the legend of the bounty hunter named Seeker grew. Few people actually believed someone like that could exist, but the stories grew anyway.

Lenora felt she was as ready as she could be. She was expecting something big, but that's not what happened. At least, it didn't look like it at first. She walked into Morty's office, smiled brightly at him and Heather, poured up a cup of coffee, then noticed the small boy sitting quietly in a chair. Heather nodded at him, so Lenora took the chair beside him and sat. "Hey there, what's up?"

"Miss, are you the bounty hunter?"

She took a long appreciative sip from her mug then nodded. "Yup, that's me. You need help finding someone?"

He nodded then pulled some money out of his pocket. "The policeman I talked to said I have to pay you with cash. I've got twelve dollars and thirty-seven cents. It's all I have left after paying for the bus ticket. Is that enough?"

Lenora was fighting to keep the smile off her face. She seriously expected to be hunting for another lost puppy or something. "Could be. Depends on who or what I have to find."

"I need to find Dougie."

"Okay, who's Dougie?"

"He's my imaginary friend. That's what everybody says, but he's not imaginary. He's real. He's real and he did a bad thing."

Lenora was paying closer attention now, her coffee all but forgotten. Her instincts were fairly singing. "Yeah? Tell me about him. What's he look like?"

"Well, he's a grown up, but he's not old. He only comes to the foster house when everybody else is asleep."

"Foster house? You're in foster care?"

"Yeah. Mom and Dad fought a lot, then Dad ran away. Mom got sick after that, and she died. They put me in a house with lots of other kids. I don't like it there. Those people are mean."

Lenora's voice took on a hard edge. "I'll talk to them. What's your name?"

"Nicky."

"Okay, Nicky, tell me about Dougie."

"He comes to talk to me when it's dark out. He comes in the room with the three of us, but only when the others are sleeping. He talks to me, but I don't think I like him. He says mean things about the older girls."

"And he did something bad? Did he hurt one of the girls?"

"I think so. The foster parents say Margaret ran away, but ..."

"You don't think so?"

"Dougie was always talking about her. It wasn't nice. I think he took her."

"Oh? What makes you think that?"

Nicky reached back into his pocket and pulled out a phone. "This is Margaret's. She's always taking selfies and stuff. She wouldn't leave this if she'd run away." His small fingers danced across the phone and a girl's face appeared. She looked about sixteen, pretty and trying too hard to look older.

Lenora took a long look at the picture then turned back to Nicky. "Tell me about Dougie. When did you first meet him? Was it when your mom and dad were fighting? After your dad left? Or was it after they put you in the foster home?"

"It was after I was put in the care home. I got up to use the bathroom and there was a guy there. I think he was stealing stuff, but he said he wasn't really there. He was just my imaginary friend."

"Does he show up every night or just sometimes?"

"Just sometimes, when he wants to steal stuff. He's really weird, he steals the girl's underwear."

"Yup, that's weird all right. Okay, Nicky. Give me a minute and I'll take a look for Margaret." She stood and set her now cold coffee on Heather's desk then stepped to an open space. "Margaret, talk to me, Margaret. Tell me where you are. Tell me where you are, sweetie. Margaret, where ... Son of a bitch. Heather, get me Andy Blaise on the phone." She still seemed to be in a slight trance. "Come on, give me the numbers. Where ... ah. Okay then."

"Here's Andy, Lennie."

Lenora took the phone from Heather and brought it to her ear. "Andy, it's Seeker. I've got something for you. There's an old house, 221 East Fourteenth. There's a teenage girl being held there. Andy, she's been brutalized badly."

"Seeker, you certain about this?"

"I am. Andy, get a move on. You can be there long before I can get there, and I don't think this gal has much time left. Consider this an anonymous tip. Oh, Andy, keep an eye out, the perp might be there too. His name is Dougie."

Lenora retrieved her coffee cup, which had somehow gone from cold and half empty to full and hot. She blew Heather a kiss then returned to her chair beside the boy. "My friend is a policeman, Ricky. He's on his way to help Margaret. Now tell me about your dad. What does he look like?"

"I have a picture." Eagerly he pulled a wrinkled picture from his pocket. It was a man and woman with a baby in her arms. "That was me when I was little. That's my dad."

"What's his name?"

"Gill. Gill Manley. I'm Ricky Manley."

"Okay, Ricky, now I'll see if I can locate your dad." She took another sip of the coffee then returned to the open space. "All right, Gill Manley, talk to me. Where are you? Come on, Gill, tell me where you are." It took her a moment, but she found him. "Cool, nice office. Now let's see where ... sweet. Gotcha."

Lenora shook off the trance and pulled out her phone. She dialed and waited. "Yes, I need to speak with Gill Manley please. What? Conference? Look, I don't give a shit if he's in surgery, this is about his son. Put him on the damn phone." She paced while she waited. "Hello, yes, are you Gill Manley? What's your son's name? Yes it is. Now listen close, deadbeat ..." Her hand accidentally hit speaker.

"Listen lady, I'm no deadbeat. I know my wife died, and I know Rickey's been dumped into foster care somewhere, but they won't tell me where. I've been searching for him for months."

"For real?"

"For real. Look, obviously you know where he is. Is he all right? Can you give me a location for him? I'll pay anything you want, just help me find my son."

"I've already been paid. Talk to your son." She took it off speaker and passed it to Ricky.

While the boy talked to his father and gave him the address of the foster home, Lenora took her coffee and settled down on the edge of Heather's desk. She took another sip. "Morty made this didn't he? Morty, you make terrible coffee."

"I know, and you cuss like a sailor. That poor receptionist. I'm sure she's completely traumatized." He was grinning at her, and she shook her finger at him.

Ricky turned and passed the phone back to Lenora. "He wants to talk to you again."

"Seeker here."

"Seeker? Look, tell me where you are, and I'll come pick up Ricky. He says you're a bounty hunter. I'll pay your fee whatever it is. Just tell me where to pick him up."

"We're in Henderson. It'll take you until tomorrow to get here. Ricky can hang out with us until you show up. Look for the offices of Morton Gluagar. We'll be here. Listen, there'll probably be a lot of paperwork and stuff for you to face."

"I know. I'll get a lawyer on it before I leave, but please don't put him back in that house. If they move him, I might never find him again."

"Ricky's my buddy, he can stay with us tonight and you can pick him up in the morning."

"Oh god, this is wonderful. What's your fee?"

"I told you, I've already been paid. Now shut the hell up and get moving." She saw Morty and Ricky looking at her. "What?"

"We're a bit grouchy this morning, aren't we?"

"PMS sucks, Morty. What else can I say?"

Heather's phone rang. She answered then passed it to Lenora. "Seeker, it's Andy. There's a problem here."

"Talk to me, Andy."

"I radioed in that I had a tip. We weren't more than two blocks away when the feds blocked the road then called us off. They say there's a white slavery ring operating out of the area and they're setting up a sting. We were told to back off. Seeker, this smells bad. Can you get that girl out?"

"Aw, for fuck sake. Yes I can, and yes I will. On my way, and we didn't have this conversation."

He chuckled. "No we didn't. I called to ask for a date, and you turned me down. That's why there's a call to you on my phone."

"You're a hard man, Andy Blaise." She turned off the phone and headed for the door.

"Lennie, wait. I'm coming with you."

"Heather, somebody has to stay with Ricky."

"Ricky can come too. He can keep Roscoe out of trouble." She swept up her purse and joined Lenora at the door. "Come on, Ricky, we're going for a ride in the camper."

As the camper left town and reached the highway Heather was on the phone again. Lenora nodded her approval as she listened to the conversation. "Hello?"

That voice sounded friendly, but it went cold instantly when Heather spoke. "Shadow, this is Heather Jones. Seeker has uncovered something that may be of interest to you. There's a white slavery ring operating out of a city near you. We tipped off the police about a captive, but the local officers were turned away by federal agents."

"This is indeed of interest to me. Are you on your way to extract a captive?"

"We are."

"Give me the location. I'll meet you there."

"That was good thinking, sweetheart, but what made you call her?"

"It's the type of thing she does, Lennie. Remember, she goes after the big guns. Feds protecting slavers is just the sort of thing she'd want to know about."

"You're right there. Heather Jones, what would I do without you?"

"Oh, you'd perish of malnutrition or worse. No doubt about it." Lenora giggled as Heather gently poked her in the ribs.

The sun was just setting when they arrived. Three blocks away, Lenora pulled over and got out. "You guys go back and find something to eat, maybe a movie for the computer. I'll call for a ride when I'm ready."

"You be careful, Lennie. Come back to me in one piece."

"I will, I promise." She smiled and waved as they drove away then started jogging towards the house where the girl Margaret was being held. The girl had lost consciousness but was still alive. Halfway there something moved in the shadows.

With a startled shriek Lenora leaped to the side. She was halfway up a wall, clinging tightly to a chimney, when she heard the giggles from the ground. "Goddamn it to hell, Seline." She dropped to the ground and shook the dust from her sleeves. "It's not funny."

Seline's giggles turned into a rich laugh. "Oh yes it is. You looked like a startled cat up there."

"Shut up. It's not funny." More giggles. "Stop it. This is serious business." Lenora was laughing too at this point.

"Okay, you're right, sis. Let's get to it. Tell me what we're facing."

"I have no idea. I know the girl is in there, unconscious. It's that gray house there. She's being held in the basement."

Seline nodded. Her vision seemed to blur for a moment then snapped back into focus. "Okay, we've got one guy in there with her and four feds watching from the house across the street."

"How do you want to do this?"

"You go in, get your girl out. I'll bully you a bit so the feds listening will believe we're not working together. I'll question the guy, then I'll take on the feds. You get your girl clear, leave the rest to me."

"You sure?"

"Yeah, I'm sure. Lennie, I'd love to have you work with me, I really would, but we have an audience this time."

"Okay, thanks, Sis. Ego all soothed. Let's get to it."

Seline morphed into Shadow wearing futuristic armor then they shifted onto combat mode. They reappeared, breathing deeply, at the side of the house. They could hear a voice coming from the basement.

"Come on, girlie, wake up. You're no fun at all when you're sleeping. Wake up and sing that pretty scream for me. Come on, you fucking slut, wake up. You gotta wake up. Shit, if that fucking monster finds you like this he'll kill me. Oh fuck, oh Christ. Shit. I'll have to kill you and find another one quick. I'll ..."

He got no further as the door burst open and a wild woman was inside. She threw him against the wall, then knelt to gently gather the girl into her arms. "Come on, sweetie. Seeker'll get you outta here and to a hospital."

"No, no, no, you're not going anywhere. You're perfect. I'll give you to the monster instead of the dead one." He had a gun pointed at Lenora, but his hand was shaking badly.

"And you'd be Dougie, I take it."

"Who the fuck are you and how do you know my name?"

"I'm called Lady Seeker. You don't need to know the rest; you've got bigger problems than me. Better run while you can."

"What the hell is that supposed to mean?"

"Look there, in the shadows. She's coming, Dougie. Lady Shadow is coming for you."

He screamed in terror and tried to shoot the apparition forming in the shadows. Unfortunately, before he could pull the trigger, something bit him on the wrist and he dropped the gun. She moved towards him then, a shadowy figure moving with a sinuous grace, dressed in metallic armor. Wide-eyed and trembling, he looked from the woman to the huge cobra that had bit him.

"The snake's venom is swift, is it not? Quite lethal as well. This is the antidote. Drink it all, every drop." She tossed the small bottle to him, and he struggled to get it open.

As he managed to get the stopper free and drink, she moved past him to face Lenora. "Seeker, I'm not entirely pleased to find you here."

"Forgive me, Lady Shadow, I have no desire to interfere. I just came for the girl."

"She is hurt badly, Seeker. Take her and go. Quickly now, this man and I have much business to discuss."

Shadow winked at Lenora as she carried the unconscious girl out of the basement. Outside she was confronted by four men with guns. "Hold it right there. Drop that woman and get on the ground face down. Do it!"

"Call an ambulance, she's badly hurt." Lenora began to gently lower Margaret to the ground.

Lenora cried out and dropped the unconscious girl as she received a blow to the side of the head from a gun. "Just shut the fuck up and do as you're told, bitch." She rolled to her feet with lightning speed, vanishing from sight. Several shots were fired before all four men lay unconscious on the ground. Lenora stood over them, bleeding from a gunshot that grazed her ribs. The wound was already healing.

A quick search turned up an FBI badge and a cell phone. She used it to call 911 for help. She then called Andy on her own phone. As she broke that connection she called out. "Shadow, we've got incoming."

Shadow came running up the stairs and out the door, calling for Aeroth. "That one dead?"

"He is, the sick and twisted scum that he was. Toss me one of those."

Lenora grabbed one of the men who was just regaining consciousness. She fairly tossed him to Shadow who threw him across the dragon's back then leaped up behind him. The great beast screamed his challenge and leaped into the air just as the ambulance rounded the corner followed closely by a police car. Lenora waved her arms to get their attention.

The medical attendants leaped from the ambulance and ran to her. "This girl is badly hurt, see to her first."

"What happened here?" asked a policeman as he reached them. "What happened to these men?"

"I came to rescue this girl. She was being held captive in the basement of that house. These men tried to stop me."

"Jesus, girl, you must be tougher than you look."

"So I've been told. Look, these guys waved around some fake ID, but no real government agent would stop me from rescuing a kidnap victim, would they?"

"What did they do? How did they try to stop you?"

"They had guns on me. One guy hit me with his gun, and another shot me. Look." She showed them the bruise where she'd been hit then she showed them where the bullet had grazed her ribs."

"That's fresh?" asked one ambulance attendant. "You sure heal fast."

"Yeah, I do at that. How's she doing? Will she make it?"

"She'll pull through. You got to her in time."

"Awesome." There were sudden groans from the ground where the three men were beginning to recover their senses. She hauled one man to his feet. "The next time you smack me upside the head I swear I'll rip your arm out by the roots. Clear?"

"Clear," he replied as he jerked his arm out of her grasp and moved away. A second police car arrived and Andy Blaise jumped out.

"Hey, Seeker, you get here in time?"

"Yeah, I did, Andy. The girl's going to make it."

"Any dead bodies around I should know about?"

"One down in the basement. Not my doing. Lady Shadow showed up too. She wasn't all that happy to see me in her business. She told me to take the girl and get out. I came up to the street and these three idiots were here pointing guns at me. We had words."

"So I see." The medic pronounced the remaining two feds as fine then the ambulance rushed away. Andy gave Lenora a doubtful look. "Lady Shadow? We talking to the bogeyman now?"

Lenora sighed and shook her head. "Andy, don't make me slap you. These two clowns, and their buddy, were watching this house for god knows how long. Up there, on the second floor, I bet you'll find a recording device and lots of recordings of what happened here tonight. You guys know there was a kidnap victim held in this house and you know these men knew about it and didn't report it."

"Now wait just a minute. I ..."

"Shut up, or I'll knock you on your ass again. As I was saying, you guys have a ton of probable cause. I'd get to that nest of theirs before some high ranking fed springs them loose and all the evidence magically disappears."

One of the other policemen stepped close and reached for her. "We'll just tuck you in the back seat of our cruiser first."

"Got a death wish, cowboy?" Lenora stepped back and assumed a fighting stance.

Andy got between them, his back to Lenora. "Easy, Seeker, easy. I'll be responsible for this one, guys. If I need you, you'll come, Seeker?"

"Sure, sweetie, any time at all."

"I wish. Okay, guys, I have her number and I know where the office that she works out of is located. We're good here. Nobody needs to get hurt."

"You're fucking serious, Blaise. Aren't you?"

"You mess with Seeker you learn fast. She'll put you down like she did these guys and not think twice about it. Come on, let's get these idiots in the cars then check out that house."

"What about the dead man she said was down stairs?" asked another.

"He's not going anywhere, is he?" Andy turned to Lenora. "Seeker ..." She was nowhere in sight. She might as well have disappeared into thin air.

Lenora came down off combat mode to find the camper right where she'd left it. "Hey, I thought I told you guys to go some place safe."

"We did, Seeker. We went for hot dogs. Roscoe tried to steal mine."

"We came back so you could find us, sweetie. Everything go okay?"

Lenora threw herself back on the bunk. "More or less. Margaret is on her way to the hospital. The ambulance guy said she be okay. You're a hero, Rickyy. Because of you, Margaret is safe, and she'll be all right. Now, about Dougie, I promise he'll never bother you again. Now we head for home so we're there when your dad arrives tomorrow."

The boy threw himself into her arms. "You're the best, Seeker, the best ever."

"Just doing my job, honey." Lenora returned his hug and lightly kissed the top of his head. "You know what? I'll bet, if we ask nice, Heather might take us for an ice cream cone. You know, to celebrate a successful mission. It's really important to celebrate every time you succeed." She smiled as she heard the engine start.

They were enjoying their ice cream, and fending off Roscoe who wanted a share, when Lenora's phone rang. Heather glanced at it, then picked it up and answered it. "Heather here."

"Heather, everything okay on your end?"

"All good here."

"Awesome. Look, we need to confer as soon as possible. Any chance you folks could pay us a visit?" Heather looked up to see Lenora smiling at her and nodding. "We have a meeting with a client tomorrow that can't be postponed, but as soon as it's finished we can head out. Will that work for you?"

"Absolutely. Bring your appetites, Debbie can work magic with a barbecue." With that she was gone.

Heather looked at Lenora. "Is that the same woman I've already met twice?"

"You met her when she's on the job. That was her when she's relaxed. Told you she's a barrel of fun when she's not ... you know."

"Wow, should be interesting. All right you two, you crash on the bunk with Roscoe and I'll drive for a while."

"Promise you'll wake me if you get tired."

"I promise."

Conference with a Barbecue

Heather stopped at a motel late that night. They got up early, had breakfast at a truck stop then continued on. It was nearly noon by the time they arrived back at the office. There was a brand new car sitting outside and a man pacing inside. "Dad!" Rickey ran into his father's arms and was scooped up and hugged tightly.

"Oh god, Ricky, it's so good to see you. I was afraid I never find you." He turned to the girls. "I have no words to express my gratitude to you people. Name your fee, I don't care what it is."

Lenora just shook her head then went for the coffee machine. She poured up a cup then turned to the father. "I told you before, I've already been paid."

"You keep saying that. May I ask who paid you?"

"I did, Dad. She's a bounty hunter. You have to pay her in cash if you want her to help you."

"Really? So, how much did you pay her?"

"Twelve dollars and thirty-seven cents. It was all I had left after I paid for the bus ticket to get here."

The man looked at Lenora again. She grinned and took a sip of her coffee. "Sliding scale. Man was willing to pay all he had, so I had to take the job, right Ricky?"

"Yeah, and I got to go too."

"Excuse me?"

"Ricky came to us because he was concerned that a girl from the foster home had been kidnapped. He wanted me to find her. I did and he was right, she'd been kidnapped. I also found the man who took her.

You were a side bonus. Ricky told me how he'd ended up in foster care and I was determined to bust your chops for abandonment."

"I didn't abandon them. She was ill, but I didn't know it. Now I realize it was the pain talking, but back then ..."

"I get that. So, job done. Take Rickey and go home, make a life together."

"How can I ever thank you people for this?"

"Pay it forward. Someday you'll get a chance to pay it forward. Do it and we're even."

"Lady Seeker, can I say goodbye to Roscoe?"

"Sure can, sweetie. Come on."

"Seeker, what did he mean, he got to go with you?"

"The girl was being held in another town. I had nobody to leave Rickey with, so we took him along. Heather took him and Roscoe for hot dogs while I went in and did the nasty. It was all over long before they got back. Look, the boy took a lot of chances to get here and find me. He put me, and thus the police, onto some serious shit. That was well worth a hot dog and a ride in the camper."

They watched Rickey wrestle with the dog for a few moments then his father bundled him into the big car and they hit the road. Lenora waved goodbye then returned to be handed a fresh cup of her favorite brew. She kissed Heather's cheek then settled into a chair to enjoy the coffee. She noticed Morty smiling at her. "What?"

"You're not so tough."

"Not a word, Mister Gluagar. Not a word."

"Lips are sealed. Now, I want a serious word with the two of you."

"What's up, Morty?"

"Winter's coming, Lennie. Are you planning to keep Heather in that old camper all winter?"

"Actually, some of those monster units we saw a few weeks ago had heating systems in them."

"You'll need a special license to drive one of those things. You got one?"

"No, I don't. I guess it's time for a look at plan B. Heather honey, would you get Mary Jo on the phone for me? Ask her if that little place next door is still for sale. If it is we'll put in an offer before we head out."

"Head out? Already?"

"Yes, Uncle Morty. We've been invited to a barbecue in North Bay." Heather smiled as she dialed the phone.

"North Bay, North Bay, oh shit, you mean ...?"

Lenora nodded her head. "Yes, her. When the lady summons it's best to make a bit of room in the old schedule. We'll only be a few days. If that changes we'll call, but I don't think it will." She saw the look on his face and relented. "She was there when I brought out the girl, Morty. She needs to know what I've learned from Ricky, what I learned during the job, and she'll want to bring me into the loop from her perspective."

"This is part of that bigger picture you warned me about, right? The thing that will always trump a bounty hunt."

"Yeah, it is. There's something going on and she'll be the one who has to deal with it. She needs to know everything I know, and if I can help her in any way, I will. I promise I'll keep Heather well back out of the action. Shadow has people she protects too. Heather will be with them."

He nodded slowly. "You know, Seeker, I've felt the world going to hell in a hand basket for years and it's still getting worse. You and your friends are trying to stop that, aren't you."

"Yeah, we are."

"How's that working out?"

"Could be better. It's a work in progress. Morty ..."

"I know, I know, if anybody asks for you, you're out of town on a hunt. Should be back in a few days."

Thanks, Morty, I appreciate that."

Heather put down the phone with a squeal of delight, then suddenly covered her mouth with her hand. "Oh shit, I didn't think ..."

"Sweetheart, what did you do? Did you buy us a house?" Heather, wide eyed, nodded slowly. "Without looking through it?" Again the slow nod. "And all we have to do is drop off a deposit before we leave, right?" Another nod. "Great, works for me."

Heather took her hand from her mouth and put her fists on her hips. "Lenora Schmidt, that was way too easy. What have you done?"

"A couple of weeks ago I asked Mary Jo to give the place the once over for me. You know, just in case. She said it's a sweet deal, the house is in great shape, but the kennels need a bit more work."

Heather, fists still on hips, was staring at her now. "And you were planning to tell me this, when exactly?"

"Well, it was sort of plan B. I kinda had my eye on one of those monsters on wheels, but Morty says I need a special license to drive one of them and ..."

She got no further as Heather flew into her arms. "You're a crazy woman, my bounty hunter. You know that?"

Lenora returned the hug, smiling. "Yeah, I've heard that. Sweetie, I was planning to discuss this with you, but Rickey showed up and things went crazy from there. It's all good. The agency is just down the street. I'll go drop a deposit on them while you restock the larder, and then we have to get on the road. We don't want to keep Lady Shadow waiting too long, do we?"

"No, we don't." Smiling brightly, Heather fled the office, heading for the grocery store.

"Smarter than I gave you credit for, Seeker."

"What'd ya mean?"

"You're planning to get her settled in a safe place, so she'll be well back from danger when you hunt the big bad."

"Saw through me, huh?"

"I did. Seeker, I doubt it'll work, but thanks for trying." Lenora kissed his cheek then headed out the door.

"ARE YOU SURE THIS IS the right place, Lennie?" Heather was peering out past the wrought iron gate and into the forest behind it. She could see nothing that spoke of a house.

"Of course I'm sure, silly beans. Just who do you think you're talking to here?"

"Oops, sorry. Of course you're sure this is where she is. My bad. Okay, buzz the gate."

Lenora leaned out the window and pushed the button. "Anybody home? Any lost travelers allowed in?"

A voice filled with mischief responded. "About time you showed up. Did you get lost?"

"Hey, I'll have you know I don't get lost, big sister." There was the sound of delighted laughter then the gate swung open. Lenora drove through and it closed behind her. The road dropped down into a gully, turned left, then rose up the other side to reveal the house.

"Holy crap, look at the size of that monster." Lenora and Heather were both staring at the gigantic house.

"It looks like a castle more than a house."

They got out of the van to the squeal of welcome from Seline. They were hugged, escorted inside, introduced to Ellen, Debbie, and Victor, then given a tour of the mansion.

The tour, barbecue, and getting-to-know-you small talk over, they settled into the living room. While the others enjoyed their wine, Lenora sipped at the coffee she'd requested. Seline smiled at her. "It's all right for you to let your hair down, you know."

"Thanks, sis, I appreciate that, but I like coffee. Alcohol's a depressant, I prefer stimulants. Gosh, you folks sure know how to live. This place is awesome."

Seline laughed. "A somewhat less than subtle change of subject, but, you're right. It's time to have that discussion. Ellen, would you like to go first, bring our guests into the loop?"

"Of course. For months now, all of us have been having a sense that some sort of doom is coming. We've redoubled our efforts to find out what it might be, but we can't find anything concrete to put a finger on. Seline?"

"I've done night patrols, Vic's done night patrols, we've terrorized the few gangs that manage to behave themselves and survive. Nothing. I asked the chief of police, and he admitted he has had similar feelings, but still nothing concrete.

"However, there is something at work here. Moragah is unclear on what it is as well, but she has warned me to stay alert. When Heather called and spoke of the feds protecting slavers I thought we had it nailed."

Lenora sighed. "But?"

"Still nothing concrete. I got nothing but inane babbling from that kidnapper, something about a monster from the river, women in plastic bags, nightmare stuff."

"How about the fed?"

"He wasn't a lot of help either. His boss said an old friend had called in a favor. They were just supposed to watch, record, and keep the locals out of the action. He didn't know any more than that. I got the name of his boss, but haven't tracked him down yet.

"Now, your turn. How did you tap into this shit?"

Lenora stood up and began to pace. "It was kinda weird, actually. There was this kid, in foster care. They said one of the older girl had run away, but Ricky didn't buy it. He skipped school and tried to tell the cops. They just laughed at him, but one of them is a friend of ours. Andy sensed something was up, but was ordered to back off. He told Ricky about me and where to find me. He put the boy on a bus to Henderson.

"Ricky's a sweet kid, and he genuinely cares about people. He told me his story about his imaginary friend who had done something bad. Turns out the imaginary friend was a psycho, probably a former member of the foster home, who occasionally broke into the place to steal the girl's undies. Rickey suspected that he'd taken the girl.

"I checked it out and the kid was right. We called Andy and told him where to find her, but the feds stopped him from interfering. That's when we called you. The rest you know."

"So, what happened to the boy?"

"I tracked down his dad and it turns out he'd been searching for the kid. That's why we had to hurry back, so he could pick up Ricky. Happy ending."

"Sweet, but it still leaves us in the dark."

Ellen had been watching Lenora. "You know, Lenora, you pace just like Seline when you're working something through your mind. Can you share?"

Lenora stopped, grinned sheepishly, then resumed her seat. "Okay. Seline, remember when you asked me to hunt for that creature?"

"Yeah. I remember you dang near choked to death on me. Not going there again."

"Actually, I think we have to."

"Talk to me, sister."

"I've learned that, when I locate someone, a piece of me is there with them. That's why I choked; they were under water. Now, here's the rub. You described the creature, but I called for Dan. He was the one Justice knew, not your old enemy."

"Shit, you should have called for Linwood."

"Exactly. Ready to try again?"

"Are you up for this? Remember the last time."

Lenora smiled reassuringly. "I'll hold my breath." She rose to her feet. "So, the name is Linwood. Got it." She started to focus. "Talk to me, Linwood. Where are you, you misbegotten son of a bitch, where are you? Linwood?" Suddenly she gulped in a big lung full of air, but released it. "So there you are. He's on a ship, talking to ... oh Jesus." She angrily shook off the trance and started to swear.

"Dirty rotten miserable bastard. I'll goddamn kill you if I get my hands on you."

Heather instantly had Lenora in her arms. "Easy, girl, easy. Deep breath now. That's it, deep breath. Now, tell us what you saw."

Lenora fought to control the rage that burned within her. Finally she spoke. "They were on a boat, pulling body bags from the water. Each bag contained a terrified girl with a breathing apparatus. They looked in the bag, resealed it, then stacked them on the deck.

"Linwood. Just as you said, big, indistinct face, humanoid body, and yet skin like a fish. It shook hands with the man on the boat and it didn't burn him. He sensed me watching and spoke one word before I broke loose. Shadow. He thought it was you."

"Where are they?" Seline had morphed into Lady Shadow.

"Too far offshore. You won't be able to get to him from here, not right now, not in time."

"Well crap." Shadow morphed back into Seline and sank into her chair. "That truly sucks. So, any suggestions?"

Ellen rose and started pacing. "All right, we now know the threat, and, apparently, it knows us. Justice can fill us in on its physical abilities. We also know now that it is somehow involved in the slavery ring. For what reasons we can't guess, but it is. From what Lenora has discovered we can assume they're taking their captives out of the cities under water."

Victor looked thoughtful. "Money used to be his great motivator, but that would be of no use to him in his current state. I wonder what's motivating him now?"

Ellen resumed her chair. "Somehow I'm sure we'll find out, and I'm equally certain we won't like it. Having said that, it sure would be nice to know. It would give us an edge."

"This doesn't make any sense at all." Now it was Heather's turn to look puzzled. "Vic, you know more about the gang mentality than any of us. What could motivate this man."

"Revenge most likely. We stopped him cold, broke his drug smuggling business, destroyed his gangs, then killed him. If this creature truly believes itself to be Linwood, he'd want revenge."

Lenora sat up straighter. "That's right. He sensed something watching him and his first thought was Shadow. He's got you guys on the brain all right. The question is, what the hell is the deal with the girls? How does this slavery ring fit into the picture?"

"Lenora's, right," sighed, Ellen. "That is indeed the key question. Anybody got any ideas?"

"I think I might."

"Heather?"

"A few years ago I was part of a group that broke up a dog fighting ring. I helped rescue the dogs. Anyway, it came out in the trial later that some of the men use the dogs like money, to buy things from the other guys. Some of the desperate confessed to stealing pit bulls from back yards and trading them to the breeders for drugs and stuff."

She had Seline's full attention. "So you think the girls are just a commodity? He's trading them for something else he wants? It makes a sick sort of sense."

"I'll bet on more."

"Ellen?"

"He's trying to get our attention. Yes, he has to steal girls to trade for something, and, as Vic says, he probably wants revenge ..."

"So, even though it would make more sense to steal the women from a safer area, he does it here. Probably gets thrill from taking them right out from under our noses."

"Already I hate this fucker and want him dead."

Heather reached for Lenora's hand. "Easy, sweetie, easy. We all do. Now that we have an idea who is behind all this we need to confirm our suspicions somehow."

Lenora was on her feet again. "I know, love, I know, but we have to put a stop to what he's doing. Jesus, we can't let him keep stealing ..."

Heather stood and gathered Lenora into her arms. "We will. We'll put a stop to him. Stay with us now. This is the part where we figure out how. Focus now. What's the next step?"

A smile began to play at Lenora's lips. "You're the brains of the outfit, you tell me."

"This isn't our gig, it's Seline's. Her enemy, her territory. I suggest we let Lady Shadow take the lead, offer any and all possible assistance, but ..."

"Let big sister take the lead?"

"Yes, Miss Independent I must Save the World, I have a sense that we have a part to play here, but only a part."

"Okay, gotcha. Taking a deep breath and stepping back."

Ellen looked puzzled. "Lenora, what triggered you? Seeing the abused women, I get that, but the power of your reaction I would expect from Kara who suffered a similar fate, but not you. Can you explain?"

Lenora sighed and relaxed, returning to her chair and pulling Heather onto her lap. "It was the fear in the girl's eyes, Ellen. She was bound, her mouth taped, and a breather on her face. It was the terror in her eyes. I've felt that fear myself too many times. Gods I wanted to spare her that."

"Can you pinpoint the boat?" Seline leaped to her feet, grabbing for her phone. "Are they still in our waters?"

"What? Oh yes, they're just outside the Cape."

"Hang on. Hello, Chief, Seline Elmore here. Listen, There's a boat just off the cape with several kidnapped women on board. It's part of a white slavery ring. Listen, here's the description of the boat." She held the phone towards Lenora who had the idea. She'd slipped into her trance again. She described the boat and gave its name. "Okay, Chief. Yes sir, all my pleasure."

Seline sighed and flopped back into her chair. "That was the chief of police. With any luck he'll get them before they reach international waters."

"He's no longer on the boat." Lenora's eyes were still focused far away. "Linwood isn't there, but the girls are. The boat's leaving, heading out to sea." She returned to the room, swearing under her breath.

"Easy, sweetie, give it a while then check again. Meanwhile, are we on board with giving Shadow the lead here? After all, we came to help."

"Maybe you did, but I came for the hot dogs." Everybody chuckled at that. "Sorry folks. I get a bit intense sometimes. I apologize for the language."

"Don't," said Vic. "I actually learned a few new ones." Debbie poked him in the ribs, and everyone laughed.

They continued to plot and plan, Ellen refreshed the drinks, but Lenora was still messed up. Twice they noticed her focusing far away. Suddenly she leaped to her feet. "Yes! Gotcha, you bastards. Oh fuck, they're throwing the women overboard. Oh god. Oh man, now there's divers in the water. It's the coast guard. They're all over that damned boat. They're bringing the girls out of the water now. Oh thank Christ."

Lenora was crying with relief now and Heather was holding her. She got control and apologized again. "Sorry folks, didn't mean to come apart on you like that."

"Don't be," said Seline, stepping closer to gently hug Lenora. "We've just seen a bit of what your powers are, some of what they cost you."

"Huh?"

"Sis, you said that a piece of you is there with the person you find. That creates a bond of sorts, good or bad. You've been brutalized and you know that fear. Seeing that girl's eyes made her a part of you, like a sister."

"Yeah, I guess. I need to toughen up I suppose."

"I'm not so sure about that. I think it's your natural compassion that allows you to hone in on these folks, it builds that connection. I'll bet the connection to the bad guys you hunt is different, but still a connection."

"Yeah, it is."

"Don't toughen up too much, sis. I swear I'll do everything in my power to make this stop, and I'll do whatever it takes to protect you. Honey, the rest of us gave up a lot of our humanity to do what we do. We've had to. I think the other priestesses would agree with me that you should hold on to your compassion."

"Look, I'm the big, bad, scary, bounty hunter. If any of you guys blow my cover and tell the world what a puss I really am, well, I won't be able to work. I'll starve, or, worse yet, I'll move in with you."

"Any time, Lenora. Any time at all." Ellen was smiling at her, and Lenora realized she meant it. Just then, Seline's phone rang. She held up a finger for silence as she put it on speaker.

"Hello. Chief?"

"We got 'em, Miss Elmore. Your tip was just in time. We caught the boat just before it reached international waters. We have eight men in custody and six young girls on their way to the hospital to get checked out, then they'll be returned to their families. Just thought you'd like to know. Can you tell me how you knew about this?"

"An informant of mine, down by the docks. Something didn't look right so he looked closer. What he saw made him sick, so he called me and I called you."

"I owe you one, Miss Elmore."

"And I will collect, Chief. G'night." She shut off the phone then turned to Lenora with a bright smile. "There, all fixed."

Lenora smiled at her. "You're amazing, you know that. Okay, that's been handled. Now what do we do?"

"Easy, we drink wine and Ellen makes a plan."

Ellen shook a finger at Seline before she spoke. "Now the detectives got to work on this, Lenora. This is happening in our territory, and we'll find out what's what. However, If you could remain close by in case we hear a name, or ..."

"Gotcha. All I need is a name or a picture, preferably both. I'll keep my phone close and the instant you have anything let me know. I can save you a lot of time tracking people down."

"There's a guest suite you guys could occupy for a while," suggested Seline.

"Actually, there's business we have to attend to in Henderson. However, it occurs to me you might want to offer that suite to Little Blue and Justice. They've had hands on experience with these things."

"That's not a bad plan," agreed Ellen. "We'll contact them tomorrow. For now, we put the word out what we're looking for."

"That'll be my job."

Seline turned to Victor. "Okay, so how come you get that job all to yourself?"

"Tell me the local gangsters wouldn't love to have the Viper owe them a favor."

"Okay, but don't make any promises you can't keep. I'll start hanging out along the docks and the river. Who knows, I might get lucky."

Debbie grinned. "I know, Ellen, I know. I'll be watching for sudden bank blips among the local toughs, gang wannabes and such. If these people are taking teenagers then it's most likely teenagers who're doing it. Who else could get close enough to a teen girl? I'll also be watching for the known pedophiles, standard creeps, etc."

Lenora nodded. "Heather and I will also be keeping an eye on Linwood. Wouldn't hurt to make him a bit nervous. I'll check up on him two or three times a day and Heather can keep me from drowning."

Seline smiled and began to relax. "We have a plan. Now only one question remains."

"What's that," asked Lenora.

"Are you guys taking Aeroth with you when you go, or am I keeping Roscoe here with us?" They turned to where she was pointing. There was the beagle, sound asleep, tucked under the dragon's wing. Aeroth raised his head, looked back at them, winked then lowered his head and went back to sleep himself.

Seeker on Watch

The next morning saw them back on the road, headed home. Lenora was being quiet and Heather was content to leave her with her own thoughts. Finally Lenora let her head rest back and called in her mind. "Lady Moragah?"

"*I am here, my daughter.*"

"Lady, about what happened last night. I really came unglued when I saw the terror in that girl's eyes."

"*You saw your sister's eyes when your father became violent?*"

"Yes. Will I ever get past that? I mean, if this is the sort of thing we'll be facing in future, shouldn't I be more like Justice so I can do my job?"

"*I offer you this, my priestess: If you had shown no emotion, no distress, would Seline have been so quick to leap to action? Would the young women then have been rescued? Lenora, it is your natural compassion that allows you to find others so easily. Heather said it best, your task is not to right all wrongs, but to help where you can, as in the case of the child, Ricky. That was well done. In the case of the creature, Linwood, help Seline all you can, but the battle is hers. If she needs help she will ask.*"

"Okay, I guess."

"*As a child you were taught that it was always your task to make things right, no matter who or what the cause. If you couldn't you were punished. Lenora, my daughter, that won't happen here. This is not your task; I only ask here that you assist Seline as best you can.*"

173

"You got it. No problem. Lady Moragah, that thing that makes me react as though everything is up to me to fix, can you dampen that down a bit for me?"

"Another tweak, as it were?"

"Yeah, you know, just a bit of fine tuning on the old seeker mother board." She smiled as she felt Moragah's mirth.

"Lenora, I do so enjoy you. Yes, breathe deeply now and I'll adjust the settings a bit for you. There, that should do it. You'll still feel the compassion, but will be able to override the emotion attached to it."

"Lady, thank you."

"All my pleasure, my daughter." Moragah sent a wave of warm loving energy through Lenora, then pulled back.

"Nice to see a smile from you. Momma Moragah make it all better?"

"Thank you, pretty lady. Yes, She made it clear that the problem was childhood conditioning. As a kid I always felt responsible for everything. If something went south and I couldn't fix it, there was hell to pay, and it was usually me who paid it. Especially if Belinda got into trouble. That's why I came unglued last night. The sight of the fear in that girl's eyes triggered a terror in my heart for both her and me."

"So you asked Moragah to turn that part of you off?"

"Yeah. She didn't want to, but She did fiddle with the settings, as She put it. I think I'm all good now. Want to stop for a hot dog?"

"No. I'll stop for a proper meal, but no junk food."

"Aw, Mom."

At Lenora's whine, Roscoe barked. Heather sighed elaborately then giggled as she pulled over. "Well, okay, maybe one hot dog, but you have to eat your salad first."

WHEN THEY GOT BACK, Heather wanted to tour the house, but Morty had a couple of jobs waiting. That ate up a week of their time.

Twice each day Lenora tuned in on Linwood. She kept it short, just a glance to get his location, but he stayed in the water, always moving. By the time they'd finished the two hunts and returned, she was getting a picture of his favorite haunts. He was staying close to the general area where the women had been rescued. She called Shadow with the information.

Lenora entered the office with Heather on her arm, wearing the blue suit that originally had captured her interest. Both were smiling. Heather settled down at her desk to record and file the receipts from the last two hunts and Lenora poured up a coffee for each of them. She settled into a chair and took a long sip from the mug. "Mmm, dang, that's good coffee, Morty. What did you do different?"

"I finally read the instructions for the machine. Stop laughing, it's not that funny."

"Oh yes it is. Morty, you're the best. Tell me you don't have any immediate work for me."

"I could make a few calls, but I've got nothing. Something tells me you're not in a hurry for more. What's up?"

"We finally get to have a look through that house we bought. It'll be a few more days before the sale is finalized, but at least we get to have a look at it."

He was grinning at her. "Aren't you supposed to look at it before you buy it?"

"That's what I thought, but Heather says that's backwards."

"Hush, both of you. Don't make me beat you up." They were both smiling at Heather, and she blushed. "God, am I never going to live that down? Lenora, stop teasing me and go deal with the camper."

"Yes dear." Lenora grinned and rose to her feet.

"The camper?"

"Drain the tanks, refill the water, fill the gas tank, check the water, oil, etc. You know, all those jobs us independent types get to do for ourselves."

"So, you get to do all those fun chores."

"I'm dressed for the office, Uncle Morty. I can't do all those chores dressed like this."

"And you know Seeker will agree to anything to see you in that suit. Girl, you're shameless."

"I know, but I had no choice. I spent all her money on a house without asking. I'm still sucking up, so I wear the suit for her. It keeps her mind off the bad things I do." She stood and approached Lenora, putting plenty of action in her walk. "You don't mind doing a few chores for me do you, sweetheart?"

"You're right, Morty, she's completely shameless."

"And you're completely besotted. You're both disgusting. I'm going over to the police station and hang out with the guys." They both laughed as he gathered up his briefcase and headed out the door. Later that afternoon they toured the property. Three days later, they signed the papers and got the keys.

Lenora continued to keep tabs on Linwood. He could sense when she was watching, but he couldn't see her. He thought it was Shadow and he began to talk to her, telling her to be patient. He would kill her in his own time. She relayed all of it to Seline.

The moving in went smooth, at least for Lenora. She had virtually nothing to bring. Heather had lost her parents' house in the financial crash before she met Lenora, but she'd managed to keep their personal belongings and her own in storage. She broke down in tears several times as she unpacked everything. Each time Lenora held her gently until the storm of emotion passed. Roscoe, on the other hand, seemed to love the place. He spent considerable time marking his new territory and patrolling it.

It was a cool autumn evening and they had invited Morty and Mary Jo for a barbecue. Darkness was falling, Lenora was at the barbecue while the others gathered close by, chatting easily. Heather was enjoying her new job as hostess to their friends when it all went to hell in a hurry.

Morty was looking towards the sky, a puzzled look on his face. "What's that, up there?"

"Up where?" asked Mary Jo. He just pointed.

The object was much closer now and she gasped in fear. "Oh my god, that can't be real ..."

Lenora quickly stepped out into the open space. "Get behind me, all of you. Now. Stay back."

"Is that a, a dragon?"

"Yes, Uncle Morty, it's a dragon and it'll have a pissed off demigod on its back. Stay back here with me. Let Lennie handle this."

From high up the beast folded its wings and plummeted towards the earth. At the last second the great wings opened with a sound like thunder. The dragon touched down lightly, but the warrior was already on the ground. She was tall with a thick braid of red hair falling over her shoulder. She was clad in bloodstained leather armor.

"Seeker, I need you. Swiftly now." She waved her hand and a man appeared. "This man is known to me as Barney Grimes. Where is he?"

Lenora looked closely at the illusion then closed her eyes. "Barney Grimes, where are you? Come on Barney, talk to me, you little shit. Where are you? Where are ... Ha, gotcha." She shook off the trance and pointed east. "That way about three miles, by the river. Red pickup truck. He's parked and waiting for something."

The illusion vanished as the warrior woman smiled with anticipation, her fangs gleaming in the fading sunlight. "And something he shall have. Well done, Seeker."

"Do you need me with you?"

"No. Attend to your guests." With that she turned and leaped to the dragon's back. It launched into the air with a scream of challenge and swiftly disappeared towards the river.

Lenora turned to see Heather trying to suppress a smile and both Morty and Mary Jo in shock. With a tiny grin, Lenora broke the spell. "Well she's in a bloodthirsty mood. I was going to offer her a hot dog."

Morty found his voice first. "Holy shit. Lennie, was that ...?"

"Lady Shadow. The woman from North Bay. Now you see why I was careful about entering her territory. It really doesn't do to piss her off." She winked at Heather as she lifted the lid on the barbecue and turned the steaks.

Mary Jo finally stopped trembling. "Lennie, was that real?"

"Yes. Lady Shadow is real, so is the dragon. She won't hurt you, Mary Jo, but she sure as hell can be scary."

"What will she do to that man?"

"There's a white slavery ring operating in the state. Shadow is after them. I'd bet old Barney has a girl tied up in that truck. Shadow will question him for sure. If he's hurt the girl she'll probably feed him to the dragon. No trial, no lawyers, just pure savage justice. Don't waste any sympathy on old Barney, just hope Shadow gets there in time."

Morty was looking at Heather. "You've seen this before, haven't you?"

"Yep, I have, Uncle Morty. It was on our second date. We went for a walk under the stars. Lennie was just about to kiss me when I saw the dragon coming. It got pretty weird from there. I thought Lennie was intense when she's on the hunt, but Shadow takes intense to a whole new level."

"Lady Shadow. I've heard about her," mused Mary Jo. "Lennie, do you know what she is? It's all over the tabloids, fallen angel, demon from hell, alien from outer space ..."

"Yes, I know what she is. And I know why she does what she does."

"Because you're just like her," said Morty. "Aren't you?"

Lenora smiled. "Not really. There's only one Lady Shadow. Yes, I have certain gifts, gifts that let me do things that nobody else can do, like find anybody, anytime, anywhere. Shadow, however, is in a league all her own."

"Heather called her a demigod."

Lenora smiled reassuringly at Mary Jo. "Yeah, that's a pretty good description."

"So, what is she really? Lennie, what exactly are you? I've always known you're different, but I've never been afraid of you. Can you tell us anything?"

"I guess I might as well. Shadow has already assumed that I have, otherwise she'd have used the phone and told me to meet her. Okay, I'm a priestess of Moragah, Goddess of Wisdom, Defender of the Weak. I was down, broken, and bleeding out when Moragah found me. She healed me and gave me super powers. I'm really strong, fast, and I can hear a conversation blocks away. I can do other stuff too. So, having said that, Shadow has super powers way beyond my scope. She's one step away from being a goddess in her own right.

"Now, about Moragah. Serving Her isn't like anything you'd recognize as a religion. She gave me powers and set me loose to defend the weak by whatever means I choose. No agenda, just deal with whatever comes along. I started bounty hunting to keep me and Roscoe in hot dogs, if you get what I mean. I also have to help the other priestesses if they ask. My skills were set to make their tasks easier for them. That's what I meant when I said I could get a call anytime that overrides anything else I might be doing.

"Now, for Shadow. Moragah made her too, but for a higher purpose, a much greater task. She gave Shadow incredible power, and those powers are still growing. She would never deliberately hurt you, but she does get intense. Far better to stay well back when she shows up."

"I certainly will," said Mary Jo, taking a sip from the wine Heather had brought her.

Morty accepted the offered beer. "Second that. Do you know what her agenda is?"

Lenora nodded. "She's here in this world to keep us from destroying ourselves, by any means necessary."

Mary Jo looked thoughtful. "Lennie, is there anything we can do to help?"

"Keep your eyes and ears open for weird shit. If I get called away ..."

Heather poked her in the ribs and grinned. "If we get called away ..."

"Told you it wouldn't work, Seeker. Don't worry, I'll keep an eye on the place for you."

Mary Jo agreed. "Me too. I expect we shouldn't say anything about this, either. After all, I wouldn't look good in a straight jacket."

"Me either," sighed Morty. He clinked his beer bottle to Mary Jo's wine glass.

They noticed Lenora gazing into space, as though listening. She nodded then stepped forward and took both Morty and Mary Jo by the hand. Suddenly they felt the vast presence of Moragah engulf them, sending waves of healing and loving energy through them.

I am Moragah. I am well pleased with you both. You offer freely to assist the priestesses who struggle against the darkness. I applaud you and I embrace you. Morton, your lungs have been healed. Mary Jo, your arthritis is no more. This I give you freely. I'll watch over you as best I can as I do all who willingly serve the priestesses. Be blessed, my children.

With that She withdrew, and Lenora released them. "So, who's for hot dogs and who for steak?" Only silence greeted her question. It took a while for the spell of awe to settle down.

The meal finished, they sat on the patio chatting. Mary Jo wondered why there were no bugs, but Morty just assumed Lenora was doing it. He had no complaints. Suddenly Lenora's phone buzzed. She glanced down then read the message aloud.

"Girl rescued, info gained. Conference needed."

"Well folks, looks like we have an appointment in North Bay. Darn, I was hoping for a week or so to enjoy our new home." Heather sighed. "Ah well, nature of the job, I guess."

They were ready to set out the next morning. Heather was behind the wheel and Lenora was just calling in Roscoe who seemed to have one more bush to anoint. Before they could depart an old car entered the driveway and Jack Longtree got out. Lenora gave him a hug then stepped back. "How'd you find us?"

"I stopped off at Mary Jo's place; she said you were here. Sorry to bust in on you like this, but I need to talk to someone who'll listen and not call the men with the straight jackets."

"Whoa, Jack. What's happened?"

"Looks like you folks are in a hurry."

"Stop stalling and talk."

He sighed deeply and looked away. "Wendigo, did you ever see a seven foot fish that could walk and talk like a man?"

"Jack?"

"I swear to god, it's true."

"I believe you, brother. Where and when did you see it?"

"Couple of days ago, up near the res. I was tailing a redneck who kept coming onto our land. I saw him by the river, waiting for something. Got a bad feeling so I slipped in closer. That's when I saw it. It came out of the water, talked to the redneck for a while, then went back into the water."

"What did you do then?"

"I came for you. Nobody else in the world would believe me if I told them. The thing is, if what I heard was right there's going to be hell to pay and soon."

"Get in the van, Jack. Heather, get us to North Bay, all possible speed."

"Aye, aye, Captain."

"What's going on, Seeker?"

"Me, and some others like me, are after those fish men. Jack, Moragah says I can trust you, so I'm going to bring you into the loop.

Once you understand who and what I am, you'll be able to get a better handle on what's going on."

By the time they reached the mansion Jack had met Moragah, and Lenora had texted a cryptic message to Seline. She was waiting for them at the door.

Vengeance is Coming

The others were gathered in the living room when Seline led them in. "Hey folks, this is Jack, Lenora's brother. This is Ellen, Debbie, and Vic."

Victor rose and shook Jack's hand. "Brother huh, well there is a strong family resemblance."

Jack chuckled. "Yeah, she's adopted." That brought a round of laughter. "It was back at the res. Lennie showed up, wouldn't take no for an answer, and it looked like she was going to make me the last of the Mohicans if they didn't let her through. Band law, only the people are allowed on band land."

"So you adopted her?"

"Had to, to save the tribe. I don't wanna be an orphan." Once again everyone was laughing.

Seline showed Jack to a chair then turned to Lenora. "Okay, conference time. After I left your place I caught that guy, found and released the girl. Hee hee. I let her drive away in the guy's truck. Told her to trash it. Anyway, when he stopped babbling and crying he told me something big was in the wind. Something about the Atlanteans rising from the deep and raining destruction down on us."

"Atlanteans?"

"That's what he said. I think that's just some of Linwood's bullshit scare tactics. He's trying to think creative and fanciful like me. Huh. The man is definitely not in my league."

"Nobody's in your league, my sister." Seline blushed and smiled.

"Aw shucks, Lennie."

Ellen smiled then spoke. "Focus, girls, focus."

Lenora responded first. "Right. Look, I think what Jack overheard has relevance here, but I've got no idea how it fits. Jack, tell us all of it now."

"Okay. I've had police training and served for a while in the city. I know how to observe, and I know when something doesn't quite smell right. A few days ago I was tailing a redneck who keeps trespassing on our land. I spotted him by the river, but something felt off. He wasn't doing anything, just sitting there waiting. I left the car and moved closer. That's when I saw it, the fish man.

"It came out of the water and walked up the bank. Called the guy by name. George Ruby. He's one of those paramilitary types. Anyway, this fish man told him to call the men together, bring all the firepower they had. Something big is about to happen. Ruby and his men are supposed to attack and occupy the res. to distract the national guard and to create a diversion."

"A diversion?" asked Ellen. "Do you know why they need a diversion?"

"I don't know how much of this is true, but the fish man said there would be a three pronged attack. First, Ruby and his men get all the attention focused on them, then this city gets blown off the map. That's supposed to pull everything away from Washington, then it gets blown halfway to Mars. That's what he said. He told Ruby to be ready in three weeks.

"That's not the worst. Ruby gave him a bag from the truck. It looked like a body bag with something alive in it. They looked in the bag and laughed. The fish man said the Turks would love it. Said the Turks will pay anything for a blonde American girl, trade anything for one. They'll even get you some old Russian nukes for a dozen girls.

"He put a breathing mask on the girl then went back underwater. Ruby drove away, and I went straight to Seeker's place. I knew nobody else would believe me."

Victor was on his feet, the Viper's armor instantly appearing. "Dirty rotten son of a bitch, the fucker is going to nuke North Bay. I don't know if I'd believe all the stuff about Washington, but I believe Linwood is nasty enough to nuke a whole city just to get back at us."

Debbie reached out to grasp his arm. "Easy lover, we're still in the planning stages here. We've got a few days. Let the armor down now, honey."

"What? Huh? Oh, sorry." The armor disappeared and he sighed as he resumed his seat. "All right, Ellen, this is where you shine. What's our move?"

"First, we need to decide if we believe this story."

Heather, looking deeply concerned, spoke up. "Can we afford to ignore it? If we prepare and it's bogus, no harm done. If it's real then shouldn't we be prepared?"

Ellen smiled at reassuringly. "You're absolutely right. We do need to prepare. Step one, we need to head off that attack on Jack's people and we need to do it quietly. The fuss there is supposed to be Linwood's signal that the coast is clear. We have to head that off to buy more time. That's step one."

"Okay, my job," said Lenora. "In a way these are my people too."

"Want some help?"

"Thanks, Viper, but Shadow will need you here."

Seline had her head tilted as though listening. She nodded in agreement then spoke. "Vic's right, sis, you'll need some help. Let me see now, how about this?" Seline waved her arm and suddenly Lenora was clad in black armor that gave off a soft glow. "Move around in it. How does it feel? Can you see in it?"

"Wow, this is amazing. Yeah, I can move easy and see fine. What is this?"

"Battle armor from a future alien world. Both Vic and I wear armor like this. Stand up Jack." Seline put him in armor too. "All right, kiddies, here's how you call the armor..."

They had a short practice session then they returned to the planning. Ellen's mind was working well out ahead of them all. "Lenora, I know you have an important job, and it will hold your attention, but ..."

"Yes, Ellen, I'll keep tabs on our buddy Linwood, and my phone in my pocket. The minute he makes a move, I'll call. I know we have to head him off before he can set the bomb. Too bad he didn't lay out a map I could see."

"The thing we have to bear in mind," said Ellen, "is that this creature isn't actually Linwood. It has many of his memories and skills, but it isn't actually him. It will make mistakes he never would."

Seline was on her feet, pacing, in full shadow mode. "Yes, of course, it let slip the plan. Linwood would never have done that. This thing probably realizes that it really isn't Linwood, but has his memories. It's just doing what it thinks he would do. However, Linwood always wanted to be smarter than everyone else. Perhaps this fish man was boasting too much."

"Yes, it made that mistake, and I'm willing to bet it will make another one," said Ellen. "Lenora, can you tune in on places as well as people?"

"Sure, if I've been there or have a good picture. Why?"

"I'll bet that thing will try to set the bomb at the place where Shadow and Viper killed Linwood."

Shadow nodded. "That would make sense. I'll escort Seeker to that place tomorrow so she can watch it for us."

"Tomorrow?"

"You can't leave for a day or so, my sister. You need to practice with the armor. I need to be confident you can bring it up instantly and hold it as long as required." Lenora nodded her agreement.

THEY STOOD IN THE STORM sewer outfall, Lenora committing the place to memory. "So this is where you brought him down?"

"Yeah, this is it. Can you do it?"

"Sure, I guess. Shouldn't be a problem, I've got it in my head now. We can go somewhere else, and I can do a test."

"Good idea, let's do that. First though, tell me what's on your mind."

"What'd ya mean?"

"Lennie, you've been walking on eggs around me all morning like I'm going to bite your head off. What's up with that, sister mine?"

"Sorry. I ..."

Seline gazed into Lenora's eyes then sighed deeply. "So, figured it out, did you?"

"Seline, I ..."

"I will never hurt you, Lennie. Never. Not you, and not any of our sisters, never a member of the bloodline. Here, give me your right hand." She placed Lenora's right hand over her heart and placed her own over Lenora's. She had morphed into Shadow. "Now, look deeply into my eyes. Speak no words, just feel me, my truth, my soul, as I do yours."

Lenora gazed into those emerald eyes and felt a sense of love, companionship, of belonging, protectiveness and more. Tears rose unbidden and she suddenly hugged the warrior elf to her. Shadow returned the hug. "I will not ever hurt you, my sister. I'll protect you with all my power as I will all the sisters and the bloodline." Shadow lightly kissed her hair then released her. Lenora was smiling now, her fears allayed.

"Thanks for that, Lady Shadow. Can I ask how long you've known yourself? Have any of the others figured it out yet?"

Shadow morphed back into Seline. "I just got it through my thick head a few weeks ago. Scares the crap out of me, sis, but it is what it is, and it can't be undone. No, Moragah said you'd be the first to puzzle it out. Keep my secret?"

"I'll try, but ..."

"Heather will drag it out of you." Seline was laughing. "Okay, but just the two of you, all right? At least for now."

"Promise. Now, let's go test my grasp on this place. Wait, let me check on Linwood first." She zoned out and turned around then started to choke. She broke the connection and shook it off. "Dirty bastard's gone deep. He's way offshore now, and there's six others with him."

"All right. We both could use a coffee, girl. I know just the place. Let's go."

THEY SAT IN A CORNER booth, sipping coffee and chatting softly. "Well?"

"Yep, I can see it clearly, it and a wider view. I'll keep an eye on it as well as on Linwood. Now, tell me more about the armor."

"Ellen's idea. I had Vic and me in leather armor. I like it, the feel, the smell, but I kept getting hurt. Ellen said to look to the future, not the past for the armor. This stuff is lighter and more flexible than the leather, plus it'll stop armor piercing rounds. It covers the whole body so there's no weaknesses. Vic and I tested it against a high powered rifle and it held up, but I have no idea what it would do against heavy artillery."

"You might consider some for Aeroth as well. You like to ride in on his back, but if you go up against some idiot with a rocket launcher or ..."

"Already done it, sis. His scales are coated in the same stuff. Speaking of armor, I guess we should be getting back for some practice."

"Right." Lenora drained her mug then started to rise. "Seline, thanks for giving Jack armor too."

"He'll need it. In fact, I intend to put armor on all the priestesses. I know everybody's powers are still growing, evolving, but a little armor couldn't hurt, right?"

"Yeah, and way easier than painting blue spirals then washing them off after. Penny almost scrubbed off half my face getting me cleaned up at first." They were still laughing as they reached the car.

That day and the next were spent planning and practice bringing up the armor. Seline couldn't resist, she gave them each a logo for the armor. Victor's had cobras and vipers on it, so Jack got an eagle in flight and Lenora got a wolf. The helmets bore the same logo.

On the third day they headed home. They worked out a story for Jack to tell the band so they would be alerted. He knew the band would want to fight, but was sure, with the promise of the Wendigo's help, they'd leave the fighting to him and only act as emergency back up.

Once they arrived back at the house, Jack drove away rather than spend the night. Roscoe took his time re-anointing his territory then they all went inside. Lenora gazed around the little house, smiling. "What is it, sweetie?"

"Huh?"

"There's been something on your mind for days now. What's bothering you?"

"Nothing at all, pretty lady. Not a thing."

"Fibber. Come on, Lennie, talk to me."

Lenora laughed with delight and pulled Heather into a hug. "She said you'd work it out of me."

"Who? Who said that?"

"Seline. I promised not to say anything to anybody else until they figured it out on their own, but she said I could tell you."

"Tell me what, sweetheart?"

"You were right about Lady Shadow."

"Explain."

"Honey, Moragah can only affect this world by acting through a human or beast. That's how it works. That's how the dark works and that's how She has to work. Moragah herself can't manifest in this realm ..."

"Except through a human. She can't take over a human, so she created one to become her in the flesh?"

"Not quite. Apparently, that's not allowed either. However, She could pick one, give her unlimited power and turn her loose. Shadow is a demigod, like you said. She's also a complete wild card. That's what will mess the most with the darkness. Moragah isn't controlling Shadow. She gave her power and a purpose, now Shadow is on her own to figure out how to get it done. She chose Seline because of her wild imagination."

"Imagination, no controls, no boundaries except those self imposed, and unlimited power. Oh, dear Jesus."

"Easy, Heather, easy. You've met them both, Seline and Shadow. Think now, how does it feel to be around them?"

Heather smiled. "Good. It feels good when we're around either one of them. Shadow is a bit intense, but Seline is a world of fun, and it feels good."

"Go deeper, sweetie."

Heather thought for a moment then smiled brightly. "Moragah. It feels sort of like it does when we connect with Moragah. Oh, not as powerful or as all encompassing, but still like Moragah. I get it. Moragah is still inside her like she is in you, a part of her still. Okay, I get it now. She's a demigod, and growing in power, but she'll always feel the influence of Moragah and be guided by that."

"Yup, you've got it. That's our big sister."

"Wow. Lennie, hold me tighter. The world just got way too big for me and it's a scary place."

Lenora, tightened her arms around her lover. "It can be for sure, but for me it's gotten a bit more secure. Up to now it's been the old greedy men with their fingers on the trigger that were the big scary monsters. Now there's a new sheriff in town. I'm actually a bit more hopeful."

Several days passed and Heather nested in their new home, bringing in some things from her past and adding new things they bought together. She was trying to make a normal life for Lenora, but the Seeker had become the watcher. She constantly checked in on Jack, then Linwood, as well as the sewers beneath the city on the coast.

Several times Heather found her practicing with the armor. It had become a natural extension of her body. Lenora also pushed harder at her training. Heather asked her about that over lunch one day.

"Sweetheart, you're pushing yourself too hard. At this rate you'll have nothing left when you need it. What's going on?"

"It's me, I'm the wrong one for this and I know it. This should be Penny or Kara, they're the warriors. I was created a hunter, to find shit, not to be a warrior, but here I am. I guess this is what it's like to fight the darkness. You don't get to choose and define your role; you just deal with whatever comes along."

"Do you want to call Penny and ..."

"No, it's way too late for that now, besides, she doesn't have armor yet. I wouldn't send her against that many guns without it. No, I just need to suck it up and deal. Dammit, Moragah was supposed to turn off the scaredy-cat part of me." Heather reached for her hand and squeezed it but said nothing. "Ah, I know. It's my job to get past the fear, She can't do it for me. I need to ..."

Suddenly she turned her head to the side as though listening. Her eyes focused far away for a moment then snapped back. She'd been holding her breath. "He's moving. It's happening now." She reached for her phone and called.

"Seline, here. What's up, sis?"

"Linwood's coming back. He and the six with him are on their way back, but they're still well out to sea. Shadow, they're dragging something big with them."

"Got it. We'll get on that from here. What's your next move?"

"I'll leave for the reservation today. Jack's got them pretty well organized and they've cooked up something big."

"Seeker, this could get out of hand for you. Know this, I need you alive. Leave Heather home when you go, and if the battle goes south on you, abandon it. Stay alive at all cost."

"Right, got it."

"I'm serious. Not all battles can be won, that's a given. I'm telling you this so you know, I need you to stay alive, and will support whatever decision you make. You are too important to me, both as a sister and as a seeker, for me to lose."

"I understand, Lady Shadow. I'll be careful and if it turns sour, I'll beat feet out of there. I promise. Lady Shadow."

"Yes?"

"Thanks for letting me help Jack's people."

"That was your decision, not mine to make, Seeker. You decided to help so I gave you armor to help you. Lenora, our task is to defend the weak. What other decision could you have made? How could I ever ask you not to do that?"

There was merriment in that voice, obviously she had morphed back into Seline again. "After all, it's what we do, right? Man, I wish I could be there to watch the faces of those fools when they come up against a priestess in full battle armor."

"You're a nut, Seline. You be careful, that monster has a nuke. We don't want that thing going off."

"No, we sure don't. Can you keep tabs on him, let me know when he's getting close?"

"Count on it, sister. I won't let you down."

"Girl, that thought never crossed my mind. Go on now. Go do your thing."

Lenora sighed as she closed the connection and dropped the phone back onto the table. "Heather, what are you doing?"

"Going to pack. We've moving out."

"No, sweetie. Not this time."

"Lenora, I'm going with you. I ..."

"No. No you're not going, not this time. Damnit, Heather, listen to me. This isn't a hunt for a runner, or a gangster with a few buddies and guns. This is a battle with a semi trained, heavily armed, militia. This one is a war, and I don't want you anywhere near it. Sweetheart, I need to know you're safe here in our little house. I won't be able to do what I have to do if I'm worried about you getting too close to the ..."

Heather laid a finger against Lenora's lips. "It's okay, my love, I get it. You're right, that will be no place for me. I'm sure Ellen and Debbie will be well back out of the action too. I'll be worried sick until I hear from you that it's over, but that's the life of a military wife. This is the same thing, I guess. Lenora Schmidt, you come back to me in one piece."

Lenora hugged her tightly. "I will, I swear I will, pretty lady. I'll leave Roscoe here with you for protection."

"Sure you won't need him with you?"

"In the early days I did. He was the only thing that could bring me out of the madness, but I've long since gained control of the noise around me. You keep our guard dog here with you where he'll be safe."

"Oh my god, Lenora, you don't expect to come back, do you? I'm not letting you ..."

"Sweet Heather, stop this now. This was always a possibility, a part of the deal. I was dying when I signed on with Moragah. Every day was a bonus from there, and every day with you has been a blessing. Look, I plan to come back, and in one piece, but if that can't happen I need to know that you and Roscoe are safe.

"Listen carefully now, if I don't come back, you go straight to Seline. Promise me now."

Heather swallowed hard then nodded. "I'll pack a bag for you. There's lots of hot dogs in the camper." She lightly kissed Lenora's cheek then hurried away to the bedroom to pack that bag. There were tears on her cheeks when she returned.

The goodbye was tearful for both of them, but by mid-afternoon Lenora was on the road. She called Jack to let him know she'd arrive late the next day. He told her to hurry it up. He'd been spying on the rednecks, and it would happen in two or three days.

Lenora arrived at the barricade and was led through. The guys there pointed her to the band office where there was a meeting for the council. Jack was speaking and was the first to see her at the door. "Hey, sis, about time you showed up. You want to tell the council of elders here what's going on?"

She smiled and walked to the front of the room. "Hi folks. Okay, here's the basics. A group of terrorists wants to take over the country."

"So, why should we care?" asked one older woman.

"I'm getting there. As best we can determine, their plan is this. A heavily armed militia group will hit this reservation sometime late today or tomorrow. The idea is to draw as much law enforcement and military attention as possible this way. The next day a nuclear bomb will explode in North Bay, drawing the rest away, and then Washington gets blown to hell. That's their plan.

"Now, here's ours. We stop them cold here at the borders to tribal lands. The militia goes no further than the barricade. Not big fuss for the media. There are other people ready to intercept the nuke and prevent its deployment. That's not our job. Our job is this, keep the greedy bastards off our land, keep our people alive."

"You talk like you're one of us, white girl."

"Yeah, I guess I do, don't I? That's all Jack's fault. He adopted me." That brought a round of laughter.

"Why are you really here, Wendigo?"

Lenora gazed all around at the old faces, and the sheriff. She smiled ruefully and let her shoulders relax. "I lost a fight, a bad one. I was down, broken, bleeding out. Finished. A powerful spirit came to me and offered me a deal. I get healed, empowered with special talents, and I have to allow that spirit to inhabit this body with me. On top of that, I have to accept a special mission in life. It was an easy choice, live or die. I took option one." There was a round chuckles and smiles at that.

"So, there I was, all brand new, strong as hell, fast as lightning, and with a single main purpose in life. Defend the weak. That's why I'm here today. You people are weak, and it's my people who made you this way. Don't get me wrong, I'm not all guilty about the past, I'm just facing the truth.

"As a people, you're weak, militarily. You're about to get attacked, and I couldn't turn away from that if I wanted to, and I don't want to. I was being a complete jerk at the barricade last time I was here, but you folks adopted me and put up with me anyway. I'm here to show that goes both ways with me. Like it or not you're my people now. I will defend you."

"Works for me. You got a plan?" The sheriff was grinning and everybody began to relax.

"Sort of. It's a work in progress. Has Jack told you about our little surprise yet?"

"Thought I'd leave that for you, sis."

"What have you told them about that?"

"Nothing at all. Your story to tell."

"Okay. My camper is right outside. Your armor is in there. Go get dressed up and come back so we can show them how it works."

He grinned and left the building. He was soon back in armor. Lenora spoke again. "This is top secret military stuff here. Full battle armor. Sheriff, pass me your gun." Puzzled, he handed it over. She took it and shot several rounds at Jack. The bullets fell to the floor in front of him. He waved then did a little dance.

"The armor is completely bulletproof. It'll even stop armor piercing rounds and more. This is experimental stuff, but I managed to score some for real life testing. So, here's my plan. I'm the one with the enhanced abilities, I'll be tending the barricade when they hit us. I'll take them on first. If I start to get bogged down, then Jack comes in behind them to mess them up some more. Any of them who get past us will be your job to bring down.

"Sheriff, it would be nice to have a second barricade for you folks to use as cover in case they get past us."

Donnie grinned. "Works for me, plus we have another surprise for them."

"Oh?"

"Yeah. When you came in, they showed you around the barricade, right?" She nodded. "That's because we dug a deep pit behind it and covered it up. Whatever they use to blast through will take a nose dive into the pit and block the road. We've got spiked strips ready to place at the sides for any that try to go around."

"Oh yeah," grinned Lenora. "I like that. So, are we all okay here?"

One older woman stood and approached Lenora, gazing into her eyes. "I had a strange dream last night. I think that spirit of yours gave it to me. In the dreams I saw many strange things, but mostly I saw you in that armor, protecting the people, preserving the land. I think I'm glad you're here."

She smiled and Lenora returned the smile. "Can any of you tell me why they're so hell bent on taking your land anyway? That's the one thing I just can't figure out here. There's lots of targets they could hit to draw attention, why massacre you people?"

"Oil," replied the old woman. "Plenty of it under the land, but we won't let them drill."

"So these idiots think that, in their new world order, they can get away with killing you all and taking the land for themselves."

"It's been done before, more than once."

"Yeah, I know, but not here, not this time. I won't let that happen. I need to focus now. I need to see what's going on in lots of places."

"You walk the unseen worlds too," nodded the old woman. "I should have guessed that. What do you need to make the medicine?"

"Just a minute or two."

Lenora smiled then her eyes focused far away. When they returned to the room she grabbed for her phone. "Shadow, they're getting close. They've broken into two groups, each pulling something big along under the water."

"All is in place here, Seeker. Can you give me a timeline?"

"Five, maybe six hours at best before they reach the cape but could be sooner. It's hard for me to judge."

"We'll be ready. Fight hard, Seeker. Come back to us in one piece."

"Count on it." Lenora sighed then faded out again. A moment later she came back into focus, smiling gently.

"Your woman is safe?"

"You're the chief, aren't you?"

"I am, yes," smiled the old woman.

"Yes, Heather is safe; I left her at home. She's worrying, but she's safe. Jack, what was that redneck's name again?"

"Ruby, George Ruby."

"George Ruby, talk to me George, where are you? Tell me where you are, George Ruby. Come on ... ah, there you are. Oh, perfect timing." She swayed gently; her eyes focused far away. No one spoke or broke the spell until she shook it off.

"Okay, folks, we've got no time to rest. They're already loading up their trucks. The fools expect to be celebrating by dark. We've got about an hour, might as well go suit up and get ready. Oh, about the armor, it's not supposed to exist, so if anyone should ever ask ..."

"It was a wendigo who took them out, right."

"That's right, Sheriff. A wendigo is a powerful spirit, bad medicine." There was a round of nervous laughter at that. She walked out and climbed into the camper. A fully armored warrior came out. The sheriff gave them a ride to the barricade then set about getting a secondary barricade ready nearer the village.

Lenora stood at the roadblock, the sun nearly down and the shadows reaching out. The waiting was getting to her, and she was trying to settle herself when Jack spoke. "Here they come, sis."

"Where?" She was peering down the road but saw nothing.

"That way, they're coming up that side road. See the dust? They'll hit the main road in a few minutes then make a straight run at us."

Lenora sighed with relief. As the action became imminent her nerves disappeared, morphed into anticipation. "All right, we can do this. We have the gear, and we have the skills. You go hide in the shadows there. I'll see if I can get their attention."

Jack moved away and took cover. By then Lenora could see the vehicles turning onto the main road into the reservation. She stepped forward and raised her hand in a signal for them to stop. She had to leap aside as the front vehicle didn't slow down. It was a snowplow, the back filled with armed men who opened fire at her.

Lenora leaped aside and easily rolled to her feet. She could feel the bullets hitting the force shield of the armor, but it was like gentle blows, easily ignored. The plow hit the barricade at full speed, smashing through. It dropped into the trap and flipped over forward launching the men in the back out into the air. Screaming and flailing, they flew through the air to land heavily, some never to rise again.

The second and third trucks smashed into the first then the rest tried to go around. The spiked strips did the job and all tires flattened suddenly, dropping the vehicles to the ground. Armed men came boiling out of the mess, spraying bullets everywhere. Suddenly there was a scream of challenge, and a ghost was among them.

Moving too fast for them to see, Lenora charged into the melee. It was difficult as they were packed tightly together and spraying weapons fire everywhere. The sheer volume of bullets hitting her armor began to take a toll, slowing her down, like wading uphill through moving water.

She ripped weapons from hands and struck savage blows, killing and maiming as she went, but they could see her now and began to focus their weapon's fire on her, slowing her down even more. She continued to attack but these men were more disciplined than she had imagined they would be. It didn't matter, she fought on.

Suddenly there was a war cry from behind as Jack waded into the fight, a gun in each hand. He didn't have her speed or strength, so he used weapons. Several men turned their attention to him and opened fire. He kept coming. When his guns were empty he whipped out knives and kept wading in. His arrival gave Lenora a small respite and she regained her momentum.

By this time the three trucks that had been at the end of the convoy had spilled out their troops. They'd spread out and concentrated fire on the two armored warriors. To their utter horror one swept up a jeep and hurled it at them then blurred out of sight as it charged in.

A blow between the shoulder blades sent Lenora face first into the dirt. Something had hit her hard. Instinct kicked in and she rolled away, turning onto her back. The second missile missed. She was instantly back on her feet, twisting out of the path of another missile. Lenora ducked behind an overturned truck then leaped away just as a missile slammed into it causing it to explode.

They struggled to reload the missile launcher, but it was too late. She was on them, ripping at them with her terrible grip and strength. Screams of terror and pain rose above the chatter of weapons fire as she tore into them. Another missile from a different direction slammed into her from behind. The armor protected her, but she was thrown several feet away.

The gunfire was slowing down now as she blurred out of sight yet again. Keeping on the move, she sought and located the man with the missile launcher. She tore it from his grasp and smashed it across his head, killing him instantly.

Jack had found a new gun, an automatic, and was returning fire. Lenora could see he was outnumbered and losing ground. She was about to wade in again when the dragon screamed. All eyes turned to the sky to see the great beast plummet toward the ground. Broad wings snapped open, and the dragon turned the dive into a level glide. Lenora grabbed Jack and dragged him out of the way.

The dragon roared again, and the armed invaders were engulfed in fire. Hellfire raged everywhere, but again the armor protected them.

The dragon turned, made another pass, then landed. A tall woman with up swept ears and long braided red hair leaped from its back and ran to Lenora who slowly sank to one knee before her. The entire village watched as the woman gently helped her to her feet. When she spoke, her voice easily carried to all the people watching from the second barricade.

"Arise, Seeker. Are you harmed?"

"I'll live, but I'm gonna be sore in the morning."

The elf laughed, the dying sunlight gleaming off her fangs. "No doubt. Seeker, you've done exceedingly well here. Rest, and then return to your home. Someone awaits you there."

"Thank you, Lady Shadow, I'll do that. Thanks for the timely rescue as well."

"Rescue? From up there it looked like you were winning. I just didn't want to be left out. All right, people. Everyone stay well back now. Aeroth and I will clean up this mess."

Lenora took Jack's arm and helped him back to the second barricade. "Stay back folks. This'll get hot." They were all moving back and away when they heard the dragon's scream of challenge once again. They turned to see it in the air, make a banking turn, rake the battlefield with dragon fire, and then fly away. When they looked the bodies had been reduced to ash and the vehicles were merely lumps of melted metal.

"First chance you get, I'd bury all that."

The chief just grinned at her. "We will, Wendigo, we will. Jack was right. Bad idea to piss off the white girl." That brought a round of laughter. "Come on. The men can get the machines and bury that mess. You and I'll go get something to eat. You need to eat, then sleep, before you start the journey home. Come on."

She led Lenora away, stopped at the camper for Lenora to change, then took her to her home. Lenora phoned Heather while the old woman prepared food for her. When they sat to the meal, Lenora felt the questions that were unspoken. "What?"

"Good question, Seeker."

"Okay, that was Lady Shadow. She lives in North Bay. I warned her about the plans to blow it up, so she owed me a favor."

"What is she?"

Lenora smiled and relaxed her shoulders. "A friend. She's a friend, but nobody's supposed to know."

The old woman nodded. "Good friend to have."

"Yes she is."

"We owe you, Seeker. The people, we owe you. If you ever need anything ..."

"There is something actually, Chief. You can accept me. I'm a friend too. That's all I ask, accept me."

"I'll talk to the people. What you ask is easy ..."

"And not so easy. I know. There's no hurry."

"No, you're one of us now, always will be. Seeker, can you tell me what happened to Jimmy Longtree?"

"Jack's story to tell."

"Okay. That's fair. You go crawl into that camper now, girl. Get some rest before you drive all that way."

Lenora smiled. "Yes ma'am. I hear and obey. Thanks for the meal, it was great."

Pieces of the Puzzle

It had been a long drive and Lenora was tired as she pulled into her own driveway. She parked beside the Mercedes and stepped down to catch Heather in her arms. She hugged her tightly while Roscoe danced around them barking and wagging his tail excitedly. Heather kissed her warmly then took her hand and led her to the living room where Ellen and Seline were waiting. Once Lenora had sunk into a comfy chair with Roscoe in her lap, Heather brought her a mug of tea.

"Everything go all right after I left?"

"Yeah. The guys worked through the night and by morning there wasn't a trace to show where a battle had been fought. I also learned why they were so hot to take over the reservation. There's oil in them thar hills, black gold.

"I left early the next morning. Seline, thanks for bailing me out. I was in over my head there."

"Ah, you didn't need me. You had it all under control."

Lenora chuckled ruefully. "Bullshit. I was getting my ass kicked. The armor did protect me perfectly, but there were just too many of them. You feel the hits from the heavier weapons like light punches. They're nothing really, and you brush them off, but enough of them together can knock you on your butt.

"They had rocket launchers too, the bastards. Those things can send you flying. I got hit a couple of times and I'll be bruised for a month."

"You took multiple hits from rocket launchers? Girl, you're tougher than you look." Seline was smiling at her like a proud sister. "I could see the whole thing from above as I flew in. You'd already taken away their mobility by destroying the vehicles, and you had ninety percent of the men dead or down."

"Sure I did."

"You did. Jesus woman. Lennie, you're amazing. Girl, you're a hunter, not a warrior. Still, you took on a bigger force than any of us has faced before, and you beat them. Honey, this should not have been your job. That was a job for a warrior."

"Yeah, well, I'd be more than happy to let someone else do it next time. Now, since you came all the way to help me, can I assume everything went well back in the city?"

"It did," replied Seline. "We'd already tipped off the chief of police. He'd made calls to people in key places. When Linwood arrived with two nukes, the navy was waiting. A lot of navy men got hurt, but they retrieved and disarmed the nukes. Two fish men are dead and the bodies probably in some secret government lab by now."

"Did Linwood survive?"

"There's no way to tell really. All I know is we beat them this time. Now comes the hard part."

"The hard part?" asked Heather.

"Yes," replied Ellen. "How did he do it? This creature who thought he was Linwood, how did he do it? Who did he make contact with, and how did he manage to put this together? Who are his contacts and what did he offer them? Finding and eliminating them is a task that falls to us."

Lenora sighed and sank deeper into her chair. "Well, we know he was selling the young women to the brothels in Turkey to buy the nukes. That might be a good starting point."

Seline grinned. "Already in the works. The director of the CIA and Shadow have an understanding. She tipped him off and he's all over that one. He'll keep Shadow in the loop. On the home front, Linwood was always working through the street gangs. Viper is working that angle.

"Now, there seems to be another issue. You said there were seven fish men, right?"

"Yup, Linwood and six more. Why?"

"Well, the navy divers were getting their asses handed to them when three more fish men appeared and sided with them. Once Linwood's crew ran for it they gave chase and disappeared. Any ideas who or what they were?"

"Not a damn one, sis. Give me a minute. Linwood? Linwood you filthy bastard, where are you? Come on Linwood you ..." She choked and broke the connection. "He's alive. Hurt, but alive. He's gone deep to heal. There are others with him."

Seline released a deep sigh. "Well, shit. That's disappointing. Ah well, nothing we can do about it now."

"No, by the looks of him he'll be out of action for a while. In the meantime, if you get a name, face, or description just let me know."

"I will, sweet sister, I will. However, next time someone else will be doing the fighting."

"Oh?"

Seline smiled with delight. "Yes. Moragah has found a warrior. Penny is already on the way to do some recruiting. The Lady has also found a watcher."

"A watcher?"

"Yes, a watcher. Kara and Tasha are making contact there. In spite of all our efforts the darkness continues to grow and now it's aware of us. Those fish men are a creation of the darkness, equal to us in strength. We believe they were created to oppose us. Moragah will make a watcher, someone with special sight, to keep an eye on the big picture as well as on individual situations. She'll also find us a warrior to lead the battles."

Lenora leaned her head back against the chair and sighed. "That would be helpful. I like the idea."

"And so say all of us," smiled Ellen. "So, on to more fun stuff. What have you guys got in the works for the next few months?"

"This is it," replied Lenora. "Just what you see here. I plan to relax and spend time with Heather, gear up for the Christmas holidays and then see what the world has to offer."

"Speaking of the holidays, would you two consider spending them in the city with us?"

Heather smiled brightly and waved her hand. "No, Ellen wait, you guys should come here. You can't draw attention to the secret mansion, but we can decorate this place to the nines. Everybody in the neighborhood knows Lennie is the scary bounty hunter, so no big risk if we light up the whole town, right? I mean we could ... Oops, there I go again."

"No sweetie, I like it. How about it, sis, you guys come out here and we'll do it up right. Yeah?"

"Works for me," grinned Seline.

"I'm in," agreed Ellen.

"What is it, Lennie? What did you just think of?"

"Huh? Oh, I just suddenly thought of the altar Justice and Kara made for Moragah. I think we should make something too, especially for the holidays."

The rest of the evening was wiled away with plans for the coming days and the joy of sharing time with good companions.

As Lenora snuggled into Heather's arms that night she sighed with contentment. Heather kissed her hair then whispered. "I love you, Lady Seeker."

"I love you to, pretty lady."

"Can you tell me what happened? Something in you has changed. Can you tell me what it is?"

"She came for me, sweetie. Lady Shadow. All my life I had to fight my own battles, take my own beatings. No one ever tried to protect me, never. Maybe she's right. Maybe I could have finished those guys, but I didn't have to. My big sister came riding in on a dragon and took out the bullies. Somehow that took away that fearful voice inside me, the one that never shuts up.

"Moragah fixed me, sweetie, but in the end, it was Shadow who saved me from myself."

Heather kissed her hair again. "Do you think Moragah planned it this way so you would know and fully trust that you belong, that you're safe to trust completely?"

"Probably. Doesn't matter as long as it worked, and it did."

Heather chuckled and hugged her gently. "Go to sleep, my fearless bounty hunter, and know I love you madly." She kissed Lenora's hair again as the girl slipped into the land of dreams. Meanwhile, in a faraway city, Lady Blue silently followed a young warrior along a darkened street.

The End

Okay, so that's not really the end. Just to prove it, here's the first chapter of the next story, Watcher and the Warrior. Enjoy.

Watcher and the Warrior

by

Prudence MacLeod

ANOTHER LONG HARD DAY finished. With a deep sigh, Lacy Bevan swept up her backpack and stepped out onto the street. Clouds and smog hung heavy in the air, but at least it wasn't raining. Glancing up she saw the figure on the roof across the street. Her stalker was still there. Great.

The streets in this part of town were littered with garbage, street people, and others. Lacy spoke to a few of the people as she made her way along. She'd been volunteering at the food bank long enough to become a familiar face. She genuinely liked a lot of these people, but not all. She'd barely gone half a block when she saw the reflection in a car window. Three men were following her. Sure, even better.

Resigned to the confrontation and wanting it as far away from her apartment as possible, Lacy stepped into an alley. The men followed. Dropping her backpack to the ground she turned to face them. "What the hell do you losers want?"

The leader swaggered forward. "Shut the fuck up, bitch. You been sending folks away to the clinics, messing with my business. Now you pay the price."

"Dream on, little boy. Not on your best day."

"I said shut the fuck up!" He stepped close and pointed a gun at her head, the barrel almost touching her skin. His world went sideways from there in a hurry. Lacy locked her thumbs together and thrust upwards, catching his wrist and forcing the gun into the air. At the same time she ducked low. The gun fired over her head as her boot connected with his balls, driving him backwards. She gripped his gun hand tightly, pulling downwards and twisting as she stepped into him and pushed. The gun fired again, but this time the bullet grazed his ribs.

Howling in pain he released his hold on the weapon. Lacy stepped back swiftly, the gun now in her hand. She jacked a fresh shell into the chamber and aimed at the three men. "So, who wants to spend forever in this stinking alley? Huh? Nobody? All right then, you fucking drug dealers get your sorry asses out of this area or next time I see you I'll use this on you."

The three men turned and fled the alley. Lacy raised her head towards the roof of the building. "That goes for you too, Stalker. I'm getting tired of you following me around. This is your final warning. Get lost."

She dropped the gun into her backpack and returned to the street. Tired from a long day she caught a bus for the four blocks to her rundown apartment building. A glance out the bus window showed her the stalker flying across the roof tops, pacing her. "Well shit. Didn't think that would stop you. Who the heck are you and why are you shadowing me?"

The stalker was a woman, that much Lacy knew from the few glimpses she's caught of the roof top runner. In truth, Lacy was getting a bit concerned. If the stalker decided to attack her it wouldn't be an easy fight. Anybody who could move like that with that kind of speed had to be tough. Ah well, she'd fought tough before.

Her homecoming didn't improve her day any. Lacy found an eviction notice taped to her door. She jerked it down and unlocked the door. The place looked like a battle had taken place. Instantly on alert she called out. "Spook? Spook, you there, sweetheart? Meaow? Spook? Come on, sweetie, come to mamma." There was no answer.

Lacy searched the apartment, but no cat was to be found. She was nearly in a panic when she spotted the note on the kitchen table.

"Bevan, I said no pets. I meant it. Animal control has the cat. You're out. Get your shit out before noon tomorrow. I will be changing the locks."

Lacy let her shoulders sag as she dropped the note back on the table. "I really hate humans." She let a tear slip from her eye then angrily brushed it aside. "Aw, Spook. I hope they find you a home where you'll get pampered the way you deserve." Lacy downed a smoothie then changed into a loose sweat suit, grabbed her gym bag, and headed out.

As she stepped through the door of the dojo the owner blocked her path, rubbing his thumb and finger together in the universal sign for money. "I told you; payday is next week."

"Sorry. No can do." He pointed to the door.

Lacy turned away towards the door. A glance through the window showed the woman on the rooftop across the street. She sighed again and stepped towards the door. "Fuck you, Gary."

"Okay, that'll buy you two weeks training time."

Lacy stopped and turned back to face him. The entire dojo had gone quiet. A smile played at the corners of her mouth. "I've got a better idea. We go three rounds, full contact. If I win, I get a year free time. You win you get what you want. Deal?" The man had gone ashen. Everyone held their breath. They all knew he dared not take the challenge. "Yeah, didn't think so." She turned back to the door, muttering softly. "Chickenshit."

Back on the street, she turned towards her apartment building. Might as well get a start on the packing, enjoy one last night in a real bed before being thrown out on the street. She was halfway there when she heard the voice behind her. "Hey baby, slow down. What's the hurry?"

There was laughter from several voices. Street gang. "Well hell, isn't this just dandy. Could this goddamn day get any worse?"

Suddenly hands grabbed her and rushed her into an alley. She didn't fight them ... at first. When they reached the end of the alley, her feet suddenly ran up the end wall, flipping her over backwards and tearing her loose from the grasping hands. Now the gang had a whirlwind to deal with. Her hands struck blows like axes, her boots cracked bone and shattered knees, jaws and ribs, but there were just too many of them.

Lacy fought on. In her rage she called out to her stalker. "Why the hell don't you come down here and give me a hand?"

"You didn't look like you wanted any help," came a voice filled with mirth. Everyone stopped and looked up. There on the edge of the roof, over twenty feet up, stood the silhouette of a woman. "All right boys, fun's over. Go home and live another day."

"And if we don't, bitch? What are you going to do about it?"

To his horror she stepped off the roof and fell to the ground, landing in an easy roll that brought her to her feet right in front of him. She was dressed in a black bodysuit that had blue spirals on it. There were spirals on her face too. "If you don't, I'll start killing and I won't stop until you're all down. Run away, or be dead. Choose now." There was the sound of a gun being cocked behind her.

Lady Blue blurred out of sight and bodies began to fly through the air. There were two gunshots, but no more. Several of the gang broke and ran, leaving her and Lacy behind with five dead bodies and three wounded unable to walk. She grabbed one and hauled him to his feet. "When the cops ask, you tell them you attacked a woman and Lady Blue took offense."

She thrust him away then ran at the wall. Three long strides up the wall, a twisting turn in the air, and she grabbed the edge of the roof, pulled herself up and over. She was gone into the shadows of the night.

Lacy scooped up her backpack and hurried out of the alley. She'd put up one hell of a fight, but she'd been finished, and she knew it. Lady Blue. Her stalker was Lady Blue. Why? Why in the name of all the gods was that nightmare stalking her. Lacy had no fear of any human, she'd fight any who came along, but legend had it Lady Blue wasn't human. She'd seen what the woman was capable of. That was not a fight Lacy was in a hurry to face.

Lacy was trembling as she reached her apartment and let herself in. Her bad knee was throbbing like fire, and she was shaking. "Shit, I hate adrenaline downers almost as much as I hate humans."

"Yeah, carb drops can suck all right." The voice had come from the bathroom. Lacy froze in place, her eyes wide. How the hell had she gotten in here? "My backpack is beside the table. There's a couple of carb drinks in it. Help yourself."

A quick glance showed up the pack. Lacy dropped her own beside it. For an instant she thought about the gun in her pack. "Take the carb drink from my pack. If you go for the gun in yours I'll take it away from you and shoot you in the ass with it." Lacy looked up to see a tall blonde smiling at her. She swallowed hard and opened the pack, removing both drinks and tossing one to the blonde.

"What are you going to do to me?"

"Not a damn thing, girl." The blonde took a long drink from the bottle then pulled out a chair and sat to the table. "I just came to talk."

Lacy sat as well. "Okay, talk's cheap. I can afford that. It's about all I can afford, but ..."

"I get that. You've had a tough day, girl. I loved the move you put on that guy with the gun, though. That rocked." The girl laughed. "Oh, and the guy at the dojo. Man, the look on his face when you offered to go a few rounds full contact. Woman, I'm quickly becoming your biggest fan."

"How do you know what I said?"

"I have special hearing. If I focus I can follow a conversation two blocks away."

"Okay. Weird, but handy. So, why have you been following me? What do you want?"

"First things first. Hi, I'm Penny. They call me Lady Blue." She offered her hand.

Lacy grinned and shook the offered hand. "I'm Lacy. The things they call me should remain unsaid."

Penny laughed at that. "All right, Lacy. Now it's time for me to confess what I've been up to. I'm recruiting. I belong to a special group of people, people with some seriously unique talents. We recently learned the hard way that we need two new people added to the group."

"I saw some of what you can do. What do you want with me?"

"We need a warrior, a real warrior. I think you're the gal for the job."

"Me? Look, even before I got my knee buggered up I wasn't in your league."

"I wasn't looking for someone who could outfight me. I was looking for a woman with the skills and the heart of a warrior. The superpowers can be had later."

"Superpowers?"

"Later. Back to your skill set. You have the fighting skills; you have the emotional control. Even outnumbered you fought on, cold, deadly, efficient. You didn't freak out; you didn't give up."

"Not in my nature."

"No, and that's full points to you. Lacy goes to the top of the list. Number two, you spotted me tailing you days ago. You didn't freak out, call the cops, try to run, or anything else. You kept an eye on me too and waited to see what was up. I like that.

"Number three, you say you hate humans, yet you work at a food bank, at a soup kitchen, and I've seen you show both compassion for, and respect to, the homeless on the street. You have humanity and compassion, but a warrior's heart. You take on the bad guys every chance you get. So, for me, you're the number one choice for the new sister. The Warrior.

"Ah, ah, ah, there's more. Now, if you're willing to listen to what is expected of the Warrior and how you're expected to do it, you get to talk to the boss. You up for that? All your questions will be answered by the Lady."

"The Lady?"

"Lady Moragah, Goddess of Wisdom, Defender of the Weak."

"A goddess?"

"Give me your hands, Miss Skeptic."

"What?"

"Give me your hands."

Slowly Lacy reached out and Penny took her hands. Instantly they were surrounded by the vast presence of Moragah. *"Relax, Lacy, my daughter. I will not harm you. As you have agreed to listen I give you a gift. Regardless of your decision to join us or not, the gift is yours. Breathe deeply now and I will repair you knee for you."*

"My knee? They said I had to get it replaced. I couldn't afford it. Ohhh ..." Lacy gasped with delight as a wave of loving energy swept through her, pausing to send tingles of delight through her battered knee. "Oh my ..."

"Lacy, your assessment of humanity is quite insightful. The problem being is, the powers of darkness hold sway over much of the world. My priestesses fight to restore the balance of light and dark as best they can, but things are changing.

"First there was Penny who sits with you. Her task is to defend the weak, defeat the bullies wherever she finds them and she has done a wonderful job of this. You have seen her in action. Penny's not a warrior, she's a defender. A small difference, but an important one.

"Second there is Kara, another defender. Allow me to show you." Lacy saw a small girl in combat fatigues charge into a street brawl, throw

bodies in all directions, scoop up a child, then run. She turned to create a wall of fire to stop her pursuers.

"*Next is Tasha, Lady Justice. Her task is to bring justice where too little exists. In this way she, too, battles the forces of darkness.*" Lacy saw a dark-haired girl with ice cold eyes step out of a wall and demolish several policemen who were beating a prisoner. When she finished they were all dead on the ground and Kara was carrying away the injured man.

Next came the Elf on the dragon's back. Lacy sucked in her breath as she saw the woman wading through gunfire to reach her target. With her captive subdued and on the dragon's back they flew away.

"*And now for Lenora, Lady Seeker. Lenora was enhanced and given special abilities to help the others. Her task is to locate the enemy, the lost, the helpless, etc. She wasn't meant to fight the hard battles, be a warrior. However, life holds many surprises. Watch now as Lenora, the least of my fighters, takes on the task of a warrior.*"

Lacy gasped as she watched the woman in black armor fight over sixty heavily armed men. She sucked in her breath as she saw her go down under that fire, only to struggle back to her feet and battle on. Her heart went out to the woman as she saw the fatigue begin to take her, and yet the courage that forced her to battle on. And then the dragon screamed its challenge. Lacy was breathing hard now, as though it was she who had fought that battle.

"*Yes, Lacy. That was a battle Lady Seeker should never have had to fight. I did not create her for that task. I can foresee a time when such battles will come to my priestesses again. I need a warrior to lead them, not a general to orchestrate a battle, but a champion to lead them.*

"*You have the skills, the discipline, and the heart of a warrior, and yet you have compassion for the weak. Above all, that is the driving motivation of all my priestesses. Defend the weak. So I ask you now, are you ready to become that which you have always wanted to be, a warrior against evil, a champion of the weak?*"

"Yes. Oh god, yes. I want in. How do I do this?"

"I will make you a priestess. You will become stronger than a dozen men, faster than you ever believed possible. You will be able to hear at great distance, climb sheer walls with ease, and so very much more. Any wounds you take will heal almost instantly. As well I will always be with you, a part of you, experiencing everything with you.

"Penny will help you learn and sharpen your new abilities, to discover what they are and how to use them. Seline will give you armor like you saw Lenora wearing. Prepare yourself now, for this process is extremely painful, but it only lasts a moment. Ready?"

"Ready." She wasn't. Every cell in her body felt like it was on fire, but she ground her teeth and only let a grunt escape her lips. The pain vanished as swiftly as it had come and a wave of warm healing energy swept through her, soothing her hurts and bringing a smile to her face.

"Welcome, Lady Warrior. I shall withdraw now to let you explore your new reality."

"Well damn, now I'm impressed."

Lacy looked bemused. "What?"

"Warrior, you're the first who hasn't screamed her lungs out when the change hits. Wow, you're tough."

"Ah, not so much. So, I have superpowers now?"

"Yup, you do. Now, I've been running around the roof tops for days and I'm beat. That couch looks good so I'm gonna crash there. We'll get some sleep then head out in the morning."

"Penny, I'm feeling wide awake."

Lacy was grinning and Penny laughed. "I suppose you want to test out that new knee, am I right?"

"Oh yeah, that and so much more."

"Well crap, no rest for the wicked. All right, missy, but you're driving in the morning. I'll be sleeping in the back seat."

"Deal. Let's go."

Don't miss out!

Visit the website below and you can sign up to receive emails whenever Prudence MacLeod publishes a new book. There's no charge and no obligation.

https://books2read.com/r/B-A-ZKBBB-BJMTC

BOOKS 2 READ

Connecting independent readers to independent writers.

Also by Prudence MacLeod

Beyond Nova
Claimstake
Red Nova

Watch for more at https://www.prudencemacleod.com/.

Telling a story is like knitting a sweater. Start with a ball of possibilities, pull out one small thread and begin. With luck and patience you will create something quite wonderful.

About the Author

On a far off windswept island Jennifer Crandall sits with her dogs and cats creating fantastic stories for all to enjoy. She publishes as JL Crandall, Prudence MacLeod, and Jenni Leigh.

Read more at https://www.prudencemacleod.com/.